"Blossom River Drive *works on so many levels— it's amazing and a joy to read.*"

— JOSH HANCOCK

BY THE SAME AUTHOR

BLOSSOM RIVER DRIVE

A Novel

RICHARD FERRI

PANHELENIC PRESS

Published by
Panhelenic Press
PMB 101
171 Main Street
Los Altos, California 94022-2912

THIS IS A HELEN E. KRUSICH BOOK

Publisher's Cataloging-in-Publication Data
Ferri, Richard (1943 -)
    Blossom River Drive: a novel / by Richard Ferri. Los Altos, Calif.:
    Panhelenic Press, 2000.

        p. cm.
    ISBN 0-9676723-0-9
        1. 1950s—California—Fiction. 2. Children—Dangerous
        Games—Fiction. 3. Parental Stress—McCarthy Era—Fiction.
        4. Loss—Betrayal—Fiction. I. Title.
PS3556.E775 B56   2000
813'.54—dc21   99-66656

Printed in the United States of America

03 02 01 00 ▼ 5 4 3 2 1

For my father, Ray Ferri (1909-1999), and my uncle, Hal Ferri (1912-1998), brothers, orphans, survivors, heroes.

BLOSSOM RIVER DRIVE

Adults who house them are gods in the lives of children. Their decisions, their caprices and failures shape a girl and boy's world, its torque and size, the space and time of the universe we diminish when we speak of *childhood*. These are thoughtless gods, gods whose whims are passionate, whose ignorance of the inner landscape of childhood is unlimited. They think nothing of separating girls and boys whose lives have become physically and imaginatively entangled; truly, they are the innocent ones—these inept deities; they don't know what they're doing.

Her name was Sharon. I have never told anyone what happened between us. On a few occasions in adulthood when I thought I had found a woman or a man I could rely on not to be prematurely judgmental, I'd risk a few words. —Have you ever heard of a girl and boy who...? —In your experience, that is, do you think it's possible for two children...? Invariably, he or she replied with an ugly grimace. And, albeit sometimes delayed, a turning away. Each relationship would discreetly end after a measured interval.

Yes, it did happen. All of it. These extraordinary experiences were shared by Sharon and me in the space of fifteen months while we lived on Blossom River Drive in Axminster, California, in 1950 and 1951.

I'm not sure why it has taken close to half a century for me to commit these memories to paper. Although gaining emotional distance has certainly been a lifelong process, there may be another explanation. I'm afraid it will strike a false note here—false to what took place between Sharon and me—to mention that part of the reason for my tardy response may be the recent loosening of public access to certain government files. But there's a touch of truth to that, too. Because part of the predicament experienced by the gods with whom we lived as children can be found, sterile and codified, in those bureaucratic pages.

But I have exaggerated the role of adults. Adults were the alpha and the omega, sure—there at the start, with an unfortunate return at the end. In the middle, Sharon and I took every advantage of their preoccupation. Or so it seems to me now. And so it may to you.

Please, try not to be too harsh in your judgement. The act of writing this has cost me dearly.

ONE

Dad did just what he said he'd do. He went into his room to write.

It was our second day in the new house.

—Sixty-seven miles to L.A., he said to mom and me. I'll type and I'll type and I'll type my way right into Hollywood— without selling out like the rest. You'll see! Everybody'll see!

And then he closed the door behind him.

Mom smiled. She was glad to see dad happy.

She had a towel tied around her head to hold back her hair while she unpacked and vacuumed, dusted and tidied up this new world for dad and me.

I went right to the brown sofa she'd just vacuumed. I dug my knees into its clean cushions. I propped my elbows on the round back which was shoved up against the big front window.

Outside, the front yard was a jungle—big green elephant leaves everywhere. Yellow flowers as big as hats sagged in the August heat. I watched for a child, any child. But even if I saw a child, what would I do?

—

School would be starting soon. I would soon get sick.

Getting sick was the one thing I was good at. Getting sick was what kept me home where mom read me adventure stories. Getting sick was turning into heroes swinging through trees on jungle vines or forcing their way across red deserts no one else had ever braved. Getting sick was the magic that kept hurt away.

I stared at the fruit trees outside, the husks of walnuts, the shells on the stone path of the front walk, the green smears where passersby had stepped on them. Squinting, I saw her step right out of a tree, walking fast on the sidewalk beyond it. Her hair was brown and almost to her shoulders. Her legs were long and her steps were smooth and perfect, strong and determined.

She was beautiful.

My hand went to my mouth. My knuckles brushed the window. It was just a tiny knock, the smallest tap. But the girl turned her head. How could she have heard so small a sound? She seemed to look straight at me through the foliage and the window. I had thought I was safe, protected.

I ducked my head down behind the back of the sofa. It smelled of the sweet perfume of my mother's neck and of disinfectant. I drew my knees up to my chest, breathing hard. I was such a terrible coward. And it was never going to change. Never, never ever.

I stayed ducked down a long time. A long time. So that she would think she had seen nothing, a mirage. It was all her imagination. No child lived in this house.

TWO

Mother stood in front of the door my father had closed behind him. Her hand seemed to graze it, her head bowed. I moved close to her. No, her fingers weren't quite touching it.

—Mom?

She didn't move at all.

—Mom?

She jumped as if I'd hit her.

—Oh..! I... I was only...

I wanted to reach out and touch her hand. I didn't. Shouldn't she know better than to just stand there like that? Shouldn't she know by now that once dad disappeared into his workroom that we wouldn't see him very often?

The next day my mother opened the front door to the first knock.

—Do you have a little boy here? I live right next door. Can he come out and play?

—

3

Mom turned her head over her left shoulder to look for me.

—David? Davy? Where did you go? There's a little girl here—

—Or I could come inside where he is. I wouldn't mind. My father lets me go into people's houses.

I thought of hiding in the closet of the room that mom was turning into my bedroom. But they would come and find me, my mother and this beautiful girl. I would be silly and dumb and embarrassed. Something would be said that would hurt so bad that I couldn't stand it.

I stood up.

—Why don't you come in, mom said. Sorry—I didn't catch your name.

—Sharon. Sharon Tammerand. My mother and father are Mr. and Mrs. Tammerand.

—Please come in, Sharon. My son must be...

—There he is. Skinny, isn't he?

My mother looked over to see the truth in what the girl said.

I knew that I was supposed to speak.

—I'm sick a lot, I said.

They were my mother's words. Maybe the doctor's. I brought them out as a shield against my own silence.

—That's why...

—Of course, silly. That's why you're so puny.

My mother smiled as if this strange girl had said something wonderful.

—I'll leave you two alone now, my mom said. Sharon, I'd like to meet your parents sometime. That is, when it's convenient for them—and for you, too, of course.

I hated my mother's politeness to this huge girl who came into a place that wasn't even my home yet and tried to catch me out and said that I was skinny.

■

Sharon stood close to me now but not too close, not quite. She seemed to be squinting at me as if I smelled or looked wrong to her.

Mom walked away, then looked back over her shoulder.

—Have fun, you two.

Sharon stared at me so directly and frankly. I did not think that children looked at each other that way. She wasn't beautiful as I'd thought. She was ugly. She had big eyes and a big nose.

—What do you do? she said.

I didn't know what she meant. I didn't do anything.

—I...I go to school.

—During the summer? Did they make you stay back or something?

—I mean, during the year. When there's school—I go.

She did not laugh. Her mouth twisted around like it was going to do a bunch of things, make sounds, say different words.

—You're funny, she said. You're serious about things. I like you, David. Let's go see your room.

Sharon put her hand against my shoulder. Not a shove or push, just a vote to go to a room I didn't really think of as mine.

We had to go past my mother who was mopping the kitchen. She kept her back turned to us, but pushed the bucket into the corner so we could get past.

We went to the back of the house into the room where there was a bed frame but no mattress. There were books stacked in one corner. In another was a box with all my dolls piled inside. My mom had put them out for Goodwill just before we left our home in Belvedere, but I made a fuss and she packed them with everything else we were going to bring along.

—Not much here.

Sharon stared at the plain brown box marked Davy's friends.

—You play with these?

I shook my head.

—Oh, of course you do. Let's see who you've got. Who's this?

I shook my head again.

—Nothing. Nobody.

These stuffed rag figures were my men, intrepid heroes who engaged in every sort of brave action, risked everything every day. They waged wars, fought each other to the death, died, came back and fought again against even more impossible odds. For me. All for me! *Nothing? Nobody?* How could I say such awful things about my men?

—This is Bozo, right?

I nodded.

—Pretty beat-up and old isn't he?

—He's the one all the others pick on, I said. He messes up and the others have to—

She nodded without waiting for me to answer.

—They beat him up all the time, I'll bet. How about—?

—Mr. Bear, I said. I call him other names too. Depending...

—Depending on the game you're playing.

She held him up over her head as if she was going to do something stupid and cruel. Then she lowered him to her chest.

—Okay, she said. Let's play.

And we did. We played all afternoon.

My mother tried to get us to eat lunch. She even brought the plates in and passed them before us, but we wouldn't break away. My mother shook her head but she didn't seem to be mad.

—You should have seen them, she told my father that evening after dinner. Just like a brother and a sister. Oh, I'm just so glad...

She seemed to fall onto my dad's chest. He patted her back as they stood there with the lacy foam of the dish soap bubbling on the backs of their hands.

—I know, he said. I know.

THREE

More than anything I liked to watch mom paint.

She was beautiful, so beautiful, even in her big thick-framed glasses, yet she never seemed to know she was.

But when she painted, it was like she couldn't help but let her body move and be the way it really wanted to be.

I'd been with her when she went to the art supply store and asked the man to cut the canvases. He wouldn't. So mom did it at home. She cut each regular-sized canvas into about ten pieces. Each piece was smaller than a little book.

She stitched each little piece of canvas to a sewing board on her lap so carefully.

Then she began to paint.

The angle of her head to the little white square made me squint. I crossed my fingers and could not look away. Mom and that little piece of canvas looked perfect. Like a floating cloud and a flying bird. Mom's bespectacled face was relaxed. Her eyes were almost closed. Then the strokes would come. They seemed to come from some other place. A place where there were other people like my mother who cared so much about everyone and everything that it hurt them all the time and made them happy, too.

She would always let me watch. She never tried to hide the painting. How these small miracles came about was as remarkable as what they finally became. The brush touched down on the little patch of canvas like falling leaves or rain. And then there was the picture.

As an adult, I remember her paintings as resembling Gauguin's later work, only better, more vivid somehow. But I was a child and her son. None of these magical canvas miniatures has survived to give validity to my memory of their splendor. I can't believe that they could be as good as my recollection of them. I can't believe they could be anything less.

I watched mom paint that great and wonderful morning for the first time on Blossom River Drive. I was so happy that what she had done on Madame O'Brian Lane in Belvedere, California, was going to continue here in Axminster. Please. Oh, please. If only she didn't have to go back to her needlework. Once she started sewing for people, there was no time for painting.

(It scared me that my mother didn't know how important it was for her to paint. It scared me maybe more than anything in my life. Everything went wrong when she didn't paint. Oh, she didn't act any differently. That was the whole point. No matter how awful mom felt, she seemed to feel that she had to act the same. But when she didn't paint, I had trouble remembering how she really looked and how beautiful she was.)

Please, I thought, please don't let that happen again.

—Sharon, do you think your father would mind if you stayed for dinner and listened to Graham's radio program with us afterwards?

-

It gave me a strange feeling when my mother and Sharon talked. Two worlds that were supposed to be always separate seemed to come together for a moment. It made me uncomfortable so that I could not look at them.

—What radio program, Mrs. DiGiorgio?

—Well, my husband writes for several shows. Tonight he has a script debuting on *X Equals Space.*

—My Daddy won't let me listen to that one. He says it's *stupid and asinine.*

My mother smiled and lifted the hem of her green skirt and rubbed her wrist with it as if she'd found a spot of dirt.

—Maybe your father wouldn't object to your listening tonight. How often does your next-door neighbor have a show on the radio?

—All right! Sharon said. I'll go tell Daddy—and I'll change my clothes, too!

My mother watched Sharon run out, slamming the door behind her. She shook her head.

—You have quite a little friend there, she said. It's sad her mother isn't around to see what a fine young lady she's turning into.

We had hamburgers on white bread with lots of butter and ketchup. That's how my dad liked it.

—Gooshy, Sharon said.

Her hamburger came apart in her hands. Butter ran down the backs of her fingers and onto her blue blouse and plaid skirt.

My mother explained about butter burgers. How to eat them and keep them from falling apart. My father, who almost never laughed, laughed all through dinner. Butter and ketchup ran down his chin. He kept dabbing it off his white T-shirt, making the mess worse.

After dinner Sharon and I played Old Maid on the kitchen

table. Then it was dark. Dad came back into the kitchen with his arms out like an actor.

—Everybody, he said. It's time. Into the living room, please. Everybody. You too, Sharon.

Once we settled down, my father turned off the lights.

—Darkness is the atmosphere for dramatic programs, he said.

He always made a little speech before they aired one of his stories.

—One listens in the dark because there is nothing to interfere with a deep appreciation of unfolding narrative—its theme, *its vision.*

He turned the radio up extra loud.

—And now, the National Broadcasting Network, in cooperation with *Thrilling Science Magazine*, presents...

A shrill sound like a drill, a rocket rising, rising into an explosion...

—*X Equals Space.* Tonight's story is *Showdown in Netherworld*, starring Forest Granville and Leslie Peterson.

—Wait a minute! Author's name's supposed to be right there. It's never at the end or in the middle. It's always at the start—right after the title!

—In the twenty-seventh century, war and madness have driven the human race underground to escape a ravaged surface. While most survivors have regressed into savagery, an heroic few strive to create a better world.

Sharon and I sat on the floor. In the darkened room we could see the tubes in the back of the radio glowing a cheerful yellow. That gentle electric warmth seemed the friendliest color in the world.

—Underwear! Sharon whispered in my ear.

It was the new game she'd made up yesterday. If one of us said *underwear*, the other had to say, *yes, I want my underwear.* If

■

he forgot to say it or couldn't say it because he had his mouth full of food or something, then he had to show his underwear.

I shook my head.

—You must listen, Mighty Lothar. The North Flagstone carvers proclaim they work twice as long as other diggers, yet receive no protection against marauding Dirt Climbers. Cyril Sancho, their leader, threatens an exodus to the great Granite Nadir if he does not see you in three days.

—Underwear!

I started to shake my head, but Sharon grabbed the belt of my pants. She had hit me before with Bozo and Little Bear. Once, she swung Bozo so hard against my nose that I saw stars. But this was the first time she'd touched me with her hands.

—Return with an answer before another Magma Shift contrives to overrun us.

—Yes, I want my underwear! I said right in her ear.

She had her hand to her mouth, but I could feel her shoulders bouncing in an effort not to let the laugh come out.

—Tell Sancho I will see him after I supervise the raising of the flagstone roofbeams of our Meeting Hall for the Tribes of Rock and Dirt. Tell him I need more time.

—They've changed it, my father said. This is *not* my script. I distinctly remember writing *brotherhood*—not *tribes*.

—Do not go, Lothar my husband. As your wife of fifteen years, I beg you to stay here at home where you are needed.

I had never felt so comfortable in the dark.

—Yes! I repeated, my lips brushing her ear. *I want my underwear!*

—Sssh, my mother whispered.

—For four long days did Lothar negotiate the narrow subterranean passages. Many dangers and treacherous dead-ends did he traverse between the kingdoms of sandstone and basalt to reach the deep flinty land of the flagstone workers.

∎

—I said *underwear*! Sharon whispered loudly, as if I had not met her demands.

A great joke! I couldn't remember ever being inside a joke before. It felt glorious.

—Davy? Please, your father is trying to listen to his story.

—It isn't even my god damn script.

—Now you come, Lothar, carrying the oak torch of peace? Now that we have conferred and voted on the weighty choice to leave your Federation of Rock Toilers and Craftsmen? We will not give into—what's that horrible sound?

—Underwear!

Sharon's breath came hard in my ear. Then the first cough of luxurious laughter.

The tubes in the back of the radio grew brighter and seemed to pulsate with warmth and contentment.

It was too much for me, and much, much too good. I felt exactly as I wanted to feel.

And then I laughed out loud.

—Davy!

—The Dirt Dwellers! They are here! They will kill us all! Run! Flee!

Sharon yanked on my belt and I laughed more.

—Brats! dad said.

I felt like I'd been slapped. I pushed Sharon away. I sat still. My father never yelled like that. He was the best dad.

—Honey, they're just children.

—And the great man-made labyrinth collapsed around them. Around Dirt Dweller and Rock Toiler alike. Blood and destruction and death. And so it was in the twenty-seventh century, that all human life on the planet earth ceased to be altogether. Except for a single man who was a Dirt Dweller and called himself Adam and a woman who was the last of the Rock Toilers who went by the name of Eve.

■

My father rose to his feet in the darkness. He stomped the floor as hard as he could with one black-shoed foot.

—I told Hendricks that I wouldn't ever give my permission for that ridiculous, hokey ending! It ruins everything! It destroys *the vision*!

I could no longer feel Sharon there in the dark. There was no breathing. No laughter muffled against her shoulder. No warmth, no motion. It was as though she had left our house. Then I remembered pushing her away.

My father switched on the lights.

He looked at me and my mother and then at Sharon. He turned his head up, eyes to the harshly-lit ceiling.

—Kay, he said. If you only knew. If you only knew how angry I am. If you only knew how I feel right now. I'm so angry I could do anything. Anything.

—Graham, darling—it's a good story.

—It was awful. Adam and Eve! What tripe! An absolute cliche—used a million times!

I looked at Sharon. She looked like someone who had never laughed. She looked like someone who never said *underwear* or tried to grab my belt.

What happened? I wanted to ask. But I was afraid that would make everything worse.

I had never felt so good, but now it was worse than gone. What happened?

—Imbeciles! my father said. God damn, stupid imbeciles.

FOUR

Three days later Sharon and I invented a game. It was near the end of summer and before school started. Before we were separated and told we couldn't play together ever again.

We were in my bedroom fighting with my men.

—Want to see a butterfly? My father calls them monarchs.

I didn't really care about butterflies, but I wanted to do whatever Sharon did.

Outside the sun shone warmly with a nice little breeze.

—See? Isn't this much better?

Sharon always seemed happy with herself when she got me out of the house.

Our yard was overgrown with weeds and plants and flowers and vegetables. There were walnut trees in the front and back but no lawn. Sharon's father had a great lawn that we rolled on sometimes when no one was looking. But our yard was fun to play in because you could hide under big elephant leaves and pretend you were in the jungle or on another planet.

Around the north side of our house a series of angled pipes

—

came out of the ground. They were painted grey and connected to two round dials covered with glass. The unit holding the dials was square and flat on top.

—Electricity, Sharon said. See the way the little hands go around like on a clock?

She was right. The small hands spun around the dial. Something was going on in there.

—Do you know anything at all about electricity?

I would not tell her because she might not like me anymore. I remembered being very young, crawling to a wall and finding a nice slot in it. Something on the floor—which I was later told was a hairpin—seemed to want to fit perfectly into the slot. And it did. It connected. They say my hand was black for days.

—No, I said. Tell me.

—Electricity is this powerful thing that you can't see. But it's there. When people are bad, they put them in chairs and kill them with electricity.

I looked again at the complex construction of pipes, the round dial faces silent and perfectly sunk into the deadly structure. I knew that what she said was true.

—This must be one of them, I said. One of the chairs.

Sharon nodded. She kept her eyes on the electric box.

—Other people know it's here, she said. But they never thought we'd find it.

—What should we do?

We knelt close to the electric box. We kept it at eye level. We kept eye contact as if at any moment it might erupt at us in a surge of highly-charged death.

Sharon pursed her lips. Insect and bird life hummed and chirped around us. We heard only the silence of electricity.

—We must see how dangerous it is so we'll know what to do with it.

Sharon was wearing a gingham dress that I liked. It had

—

bands of yellow and blue and green and red, each separated by a thin white stripe. From a distance it almost looked white. Up close the colors were so beautiful. I wanted to touch the material when she wasn't looking.

Rising from her knees, Sharon smoothed her gingham dress behind her. She turned her back to the electric seat. She took one little sliding back step and then another. She sat down carefully.

I held my breath. I had never seen anything so brave in my life.

—You're... I said.

Sharon stood up. She sighed, then knelt beside me, whispering as if the machine might hear.

—It's safe. For now.

She let her voice trail off.

I hadn't known I was holding my breath. I let out old air, gulped in new. Sharon studied me for a second. A sweet look came over her face.

—Yes, she said. Sometimes it's safe. But sometimes it isn't! We have to find out when it's dangerous and can kill a person. So we can warn the others.

I had never seen anyone so magnificent and intrepid.

—Do you... Do you think anyone else knows about this?

Sharon frowned.

—Everyone is supposed to know to stay away. No one comes near it.

—But what if—?

—What if one of us is killed?

Sharon stood up and stepped to one side of the meter, examining it, reaching out, but not quite touching. Then she paced quietly to the other side.

She kept looking at the electric unit.

—If one of us is killed, the other must not get shocked by

the electricity. That way, he can go and bring back whatever is needed to help the dead one. And the one getting help must always come back, no matter what horrible things happen to him. He must always come back.

I knew the moment I heard those words that Sharon was right. I don't know how she knew such things, but I recognized that she had an extraordinary knowledge of the secret inner world.

—Oh, she said. I think I'll just rest here a moment.

Oh, no! I knew what was happening. Sharon was tired now. Her powers had slipped. She had lost her ability to tell that the electrical unit was no longer safe.

It was active! Lethal!

Sharon sat.

—Oh, she said. Oh. Oh, no. Oh, no!

Her shoulders slumped. Her head dropped. Her whole body sagged there on that terrible grey box.

The wind blew through the walnut trees. Sharon was in full shadow, but when I stood the sun fell on me through the leaves and the wind. There was a sighing sound like the end of everything. I couldn't move.

Sharon was dead, but words came through her mouth, like the voice of a storyteller on an adventure program.

—You must go for help. You must save Sharon. She is handcuffed by her hands and feet to this electric chair. You may take a long, long time. Hours or days. But you must bring back whatever it is that will help her. If you are too late, then you must bury her.

I took one last look at Sharon's dead body and walked around the side of the house. I sat in the sun on the wooden steps of our back porch. My mother walked past me to hang sagging wet clothes on the long wire line suspended between fences.

—Where's Sharon? Aren't you two playing today?

I looked at mom. What if she walked around to the side of the house and saw Sharon dead?

—Did you two have a fight? Oh, well, you'll make up. You're good friends. Good friends always make up.

My mother made two trips with baskets of wet clothes. When the coast was clear, I slipped back to the side of the house.

Sharon was slumped on the electrical setup exactly as she had been when I left her.

—I'm back. I brought something to save you.

I knelt and released the metal shackles that held her legs.

—There. Now you're alive.

But Sharon didn't move. She was really dead.

—You came back too soon, said the voice in Sharon's mouth. You must travel farther away and take longer to find the real good help. You must not stop until you go there and find it, so many miles away. It may take you weeks, months, years, centuries. Never stop. Never...

The voice trailed off. Sharon would be dead until I came back from that far place.

I sat in the sun on the back porch steps. It got hot. I had to go farther. I climbed the shaky wooden steps down to the dark basement. I pulled the little rivet cord that made the naked light bulb dance and flicker. My dad said not to play down there. The dirt had a funny smell. Dad said that the house was very old so that the dirt must be old, too. How old? Maybe it had part of the secret. I chipped away a chunk and put it in my pocket.

I went back up the stairs, but I knew it was still too soon.

My room was now starting to look like my old room, with my men lined up on the bed and comic books and magazines in a nice rack someone had given my dad at a store where he once worked.

—

On my bed was the comic book Sharon gave me to read. I always read funny books, but this was different. On the cover was a woman with black hair with her mouth open as if something was hurting her and she was running from something. I opened it and began to read. The woman knew one man and another and one woman and another. She said words to one woman and then to one man. It was daytime and she was in a beautiful house with a staircase and somehow her hair caught on fire. She ran through the beautiful house with her hair on fire. She ran and ran and ran and no one put out the fire. Her mouth was open and she was screaming Aiiieee! in the round word-circle above her head. She never stopped screaming. I closed the book because I was imagining how much that would hurt and how mean it was. I couldn't stand to keep that comic book open with the picture of the woman with burning hair. I turned it face down on my bed.

I lay on my back and looked at the ceiling. The plaster had cracks and plains, cities, people, mountains, streams, forests, castles, volcanos, and creatures roaming everywhere. It took a long time to learn how to get around all the hazards and dangers in such a vast land. I figured out the best routes, which I traveled many times on many missions.

Then I remembered Sharon.

I raced from my room out the back porch and down the steps and around the side of the house.

Sharon was still in the shade sitting slumped on the electricity. Her body had not moved. She was still dead.

I took hold of her shoulders. I removed the shackles.

—There!

Her body slid right off the electric meter and rolled to the ground. Her pretty fresh gingham dress lay around her spread out on the dirt. She wasn't moving. She didn't breathe.

—Sharon is dead, came the voice. You almost saved her, but

you were one minute late. Now that she is dead, you must bury her.

I knelt at her shoulders and stared at her dead body. I wanted to make her get up. I grabbed an arm, pulled.

—No! the voice whisper shouted. No. You must bury her. Quickly! Quickly! It is her only chance! Bury her and go away and find help and come back and dig her up and save her.

I stood and looked down at Sharon's unmoving form. Normally she was taller. But now, I was a giant, a powerful giant. She was in my power. I could do anything I wanted. Except that she needed my help. I was powerful—but something was more important than that.

—I'll bury Sharon, I said. I'll bury her and go far away and find what I need to save her and then I'll come back and dig her up. I'm burying her right now.

With my hands as scoops, I shoveled air one spadeful after the other until Sharon was completely buried.

—There!

I slapped my hands together.

—There—she's buried. Now I'm leaving to save her.

I returned to the steps, then to my room. I was very conscious of time passing in an unusual way. It was not boring to kill this particular time. It was more exciting the longer I waited—and more wonderful.

It was late afternoon when I returned to the side of the house. Probably Sharon was gone by now, bored or angry or having decided that everything we were doing was stupid and there must be something better to do with a summer day or somebody better to play with.

The gingham dress was there. In the dirt. And Sharon was in it.

I stood over her.

—I've traveled very far and had many adventures. I had to

fight many people and monsters. I had to climb mountains and go under oceans. I have brought back the secret. But I see that Sharon is dead and I'm too late. But I am going to dig her up anyway.

I waited for the voice from her mouth, but it was silent.

My hands worked furiously at the heaped tonnage of air, uncovering her, revealing her, exposing her once again to light and life.

—Now I have dug up Sharon. And she is still dead. Now I will carry her body...

I pantomimed carrying her body. She was too heavy for me. I put my arms around her and made marching sounds with my mouth.

—I have carried her here and now I will tell her the secret.

I whispered in her ear as she had mine that night we listened to my father's radio program. My own courage frightened me and I pulled back from the words—

Sharon's head lifted. She smiled.

—You saved me. I'm alive again!

Just like that Sharon jumped straight up to her feet and stood steady as a rock.

—Now it's your turn, David.

We called the game I-buried-you-and-you-buried-me. I did take my turn sitting on the electric chair. And Sharon went away—and came back. I had to be buried. When she came back again, she dug me up and brought me back to life.

Many complications arose in the days that followed. Once we both died together. The voice came from her mouth and also from mine. The different voices argued about who had to come back to life to save the other.

The game became everything to us in those last days of summer.

I enjoyed both sides, being electrocuted and saving Sharon.

But each of us seemed to want to die all the time. And Sharon would never go and stay away as long as I wanted her to. She always wanted to come back in a few minutes so it would be her turn to die again. But that was okay, because I loved saving her.

The truth is that the first time was the best. But the game was always satisfying in some strange way. Even in the short-hand versions that we finally worked out—rapid-fire death and burial and saving.

Maybe it was because we both started to get a little bored that we let Mr. Tammerand catch us. We'd had a close call a few days before when Sharon's brother Rodney saw her digging me up when I was dead. He walked at me as he always did, right at me, so that I had to scamper up and jump aside. Then he laughed and left.

It was late in the afternoon and Mr. Tammerand was in his dark blue suit, already home from work from the bank. Maybe we even heard him calling before he came around the corner.

—What are you two doing? Sharon, what are you doing lying in the dirt?

—Nothing, Daddy.

He raised his hand in a funny way, then glanced at me. He turned his wrist this way and that as if to see if his watch was working.

—Come with me right now, Sharon.

She followed her father. She walked behind him in a way that bothered me. Her face, her nose and mouth, were almost pressed against his lower back. If he'd stopped, she'd have run into him.

I followed a little behind. I thought to make this part of our game. Was she hoping the same, to include her father somehow without his knowing it? How would it come out? I didn't want to miss anything.

I hid in the bushes outside his bedroom window.

—What in heaven's name were you doing, Sharon? You know what I've told you about that boy.

—We were just playing.

—Playing what? It didn't look like any game to me.

—Playing I-buried-you-and-you-buried-me. It's just a game we made up.

—A game? How do you play this game of yours?

—Oh, it's just stupid.

—What were you doing on the ground, Sharon? If you've told that brat anything about...

—I was pretending that I was dead.

—What? You were pretending to be dead? That's morbid! That's horrible!

—We just pretend we get electrocuted and then bury each other. That's all.

—I knew there was something wrong with that DiGiorgio boy. There's something wrong with all three of them—the boy, that mother—always smiling like she's drunk or something, and that so-called father who never works, never even leaves the house. They're peculiar and not quite right. I forbid you to play with David ever again.

—Yes, father.

—How can I ever treat you like an adult and trust you with our secrets if you're carrying on with that snotty little sissy? Were you going to tell me about this? Well, were you?

Something had gone wrong. This was not part of the game.

I left the bushes. I didn't care who saw me. I didn't care who ever saw me ever.

It was a bright hot windy day that gobbled up color. Everything seemed so dark.

Mom was at the kitchen table. She had one needle in her teeth, while she slipped another into a pair of pants.

—Darling, you look upset. Are you and Sharon fighting?

My mother had started taking in sewing again. It seemed like she spent more time at it each day. How many days now since she even tried to paint?

I nodded.

Mom dropped the tangle of thread and cloth. She knelt beside me.

—Honey? Davy? She'll come back. Everything'll be as good as new again—you'll see.

FIVE

The first day of school arrived. Time for me to get sick. Mom would read to me for an hour and then excuse herself to check on dad. I wished that he had a place away from the house to go and write so that mom and I wouldn't have to be interrupted.

I walked through the kitchen one morning and saw mom standing in the hallway. She wasn't facing dad's closed door exactly—more like a spot between his door and the front door. She was standing funny.

Mom did everything for me. I never thought of doing anything for her.

But as she stood there staring at the wall where there wasn't any door or anything except an empty shelf, something about her head and shoulders and body made me go up to her.

I tiptoed because I was afraid I might scare her. She seemed so deep in thought.

Maybe I stopped two or three feet behind her. My mother did everything for me and dad and did it so nicely that we never noticed that it was done. Now she had stopped and was-

■

n't moving. But it was something more than that. I listened. No, she wasn't crying. She didn't make any kind of sound at all, not even breathing. And now I could see that her chest didn't move up and down or any way at all.

I shook her sleeve.

—What're you..? I said. What're you..?

She looked down and smiled at me and put her hand on top of my head. Still her chest didn't move. Then her head tilted and she looked off toward the front window where morning sun was coming through the drapes. And she took a little breath. Just a little sip of air. It seemed to power her smile, which got larger as she cupped the back of my head and pressed me against her hip.

(From that day on I would check her. I would look to see that her chest was moving, that she didn't let herself get so deep in thought that she forgot to breathe. And whenever it crossed my mind, I'd remind myself, too.)

Mom and I stopped on the broken sidewalk within sight of the two-story Axminster Elementary School. School had been in session for two weeks and mom insisted that I was well enough to be enrolled. I was still not allowed to play with Sharon. Mom seemed to bring it up every day.

—Mr. Tammerand says he can't imagine what you children were doing. He said he couldn't imagine his daughter doing something so...

The roots of the big green fruit trees came up under our feet through the concrete. Mom didn't seem to want to go one step closer to the ugly building than I did.

She shook her head.

—He doesn't seem to understand that children don't... Come on, honey, let's get you started.

-

My new school was massive, like a maze. It was the biggest, ugliest building I had ever seen. If ever there was a building that looked terrible and dangerous to go inside, that was it. Mom coaxed me into climbing the cement steps. She filled out papers and told me to be good. I went with the secretary lady who walked me to a classroom where thirty kids sat as a group. I kept my head lowered so that I couldn't see what their eyes revealed about their knowledge of newcomers.

It terrified me to be singled out as the new kid and be made to stand up while my name was said. Why did Sharon have to be a year ahead of me?

I was often lost, my stupid confused face causing laughter that carried me from room to room until I finally lodged in the right seat.

One cold morning, all the fourth graders were lined up and marched up the bowed stairs. We went single-file into a room that smelled like a hospital, only stronger and worse. A scowling woman in a white uniform watched us. There was a brown pleated curtain. When the next child in line came to it, the curtain opened, the child went in, and the curtain closed.

What was happening behind that horrible brown curtain? It was strange, unnerving. What were they doing to the children in there?

There were no sounds for the first few minutes. Then a little cry of pain came from behind the curtain. The big redheaded boy who rushed out, a semi-bully a head taller than me, was crying, holding his arm. They had done something terrible to him.

I looked around at the other children. They stared into space. They seemed completely unaware that anything was wrong. What were they thinking? Didn't they realize that the shortening line was leading them to some unknown torture worse than anything they had ever faced before in their lives?

A girl with long straight blonde hair went in. Ahead of me

was a boy with almost no hair and a girl in a green skirt and white blouse. Two to go, then me.

The girl with blonde hair came out, her downturned face covered by the crook of her arm which muffled her sobbing.

It was really going to happen. This terrible thing. I knew I could not survive it. No, if it did this to the others, I would not survive.

—No, no! I'm not going in there!

I looked around for a way out. The big woman in white looked around with me. Her scowl grew huge.

—I won't go in there! I won't go in there!

I tried to step out of line.

The big woman grabbed me by the shoulders.

—Quiet, you. Quiet right now.

—No, no! I won't go! I won't go in there!

Her face twisted right down into mime.

—Sssh, you!

I was yanked out of line.

—You're scaring the children, you rotten little... You're scaring the other children!

She grabbed my arms and lifted me off my feet.

Brief humiliation as eyes turned my way. Anything was better than being in that line that shortened one child at a time. The huge angry woman carried me into a side room and put me in a closet-sized cubicle with a white curtain. She made me sit on a wooden stool with three legs and ordered me to wait and not move.

—Stay here. I'll be back for you.

Silence. Okay. But what was going to happen to me now?

Sharon would have known what to do. I imagined her sneaking in to be with me. Together we invented an elaborate plan to escape these women in white—and everything in the world that hurt and was mean.

-

I never did find out what was behind that brown curtain in the other room. A man in a white coat worn over a brown suit came into my little cubicle. He did not speak to me. He produced a needle and a tiny capped bottle and gently rubbed my arm. Then he put the needle in where he'd rubbed.

I was told to return to my classroom. I got lost. I opened a closet with mops and brooms and the musty smell of dirty water in a bucket. I closed it quickly before someone yelled at me. The hallways were empty. No kids. No grown-ups. At last I found room number forty-three. I peeked in.

Every other child was back at work.

—Come in, David. Sit down. The nurse told me all about it.

Everyone watched me walk all the way back to my seat.

Sharon met me that day after school. She was out of breath.

—I heard what that nurse did to you.

—Really?

—She's evil, Sharon said. She's an evil woman and everybody knows it. David...are you mad at me?

I shook my head.

—I'm sorry, she said. Really I am.

I don't know what got into me, but I took her hand and held it. I had never done such a thing.

Suddenly Sharon looked terrible, as though she were sick to her stomach.

—I'm going to kill her, she said. I'm going to kill that nurse! I'm going to wait and wait and when she thinks it's safe I'm going to kill her dead!

Every morning, Sharon waited for me around the corner by the little grocery store and walked me the rest of the way to school. We walked home together, separating at the same point. We were still not allowed to play.

—I'll get her for you. And believe me, I'll make her pay for this. I know what adults can do and what they can't.

I kept the black viewer to my eyes sometimes for hours. Inside it, in three dimensions, I saw scenes that stayed still as long as I wanted, wonderful and clear. Sandstone cities cut into the face of cliffs, a pretty woman holding a rope with one hand while she skied on water, a city shown from the air. I studied each picture until I became a part of the panorama and it became part of me.

Mainly I loved to see the ones with made-up characters and scenes. Figures in action on amazing landscapes. My very favorite centered around a little figure with a pipe-cleaner body and a tiny light bulb head who went to strange and amazing planets. He was almost always alone, but the vistas he occupied seemed fuller than anything crowded with people could ever be. He was different and peculiar, but he went to all these great places in space. He could go anywhere, it seemed. I especially liked the little round worlds he stood on, so small that you could see them curving away beneath his feet. The night sky was pitch black, the stars bright little pin-pricks of light that were painfully beautiful.

For hours, I was that little man and he was me. We could go anywhere. We could do anything.

—What's wrong with you?

It was a shock to see anyone other than mom or dad looming over me in my bed.

—I'm sick, I said.

Sharon put her hands on her hips and considered. Then she folded her arms across her chest.

—You don't look sick to me.

—I don't?

I'd woken up early and decided I didn't feel good. Not good enough to face school. I always ran a temperature, always had some sort of junk in my chest, so it wasn't hard to convince myself first and then my mother that I was too sick to go to Axminster Elementary.

—No, Sharon said. You don't at all. And I have something great to show you if you'll hurry up and get dressed and walk with me.

I went up on an elbow.

I couldn't believe it. She actually had me considering getting up and going out with her.

—Remember that nurse? Sharon said. If you hurry up and get ready, I'll show you how we're going to get her. Come on. You're not sick. You're never sick.

I pulled on my pants, pulled my shirt over the top. At first I felt like a prisoner being taken away. Then, when I got my shoes on, I felt so good I couldn't believe it.

Sharon was right. I wasn't sick.

—Mom, I...

—Sharon told me, honey. I'm proud of you for wanting to go to school despite your little sniffle. I know you'll do great on your big test.

Mom turned her head away as if someone had called her. She looked back at me with her wonderful smile.

I stared at her. Now I wanted to stay home. I wanted to stay home and be read to and...

—Davy, you slow poke! Come on!

We were halfway to school when Sharon stopped at Mrs. Mary Proselwhite's house. At least, that's what was painted in orange and blue and green and yellow on a wooden sign with hummingbirds and clouds that hung on the front porch. We picked a corner of the lawn where we couldn't be seen from any of the side windows.

Sharon undid a sweater button to show me what she had hidden. I couldn't have been more shocked if it had been some deadly snake. To this day, I don't know where Sharon found a hypodermic syringe. She explained in detail the vile ingredients she planned to put in it. She described how she would stab the nurse with the sharp needle and inject her when she wasn't looking.

—Okay, I said and started to walk again.

But Sharon stopped me with both hands on my hips.

—Be quiet, she said.

—I wasn't saying...

—I've got a secret, Sharon said. A big secret.

—Tell me.

—No. You're not ready yet. Maybe you'll never be ready.

I pulled back. I didn't like her hands on my hips like that. It felt like I was her child or a doll she was playing with.

—Actually, she said. You will be ready. One day. I don't know when, but I'm sure I can count on you.

A warm wind made Mrs. Proselwhite's sign swing a little.

—I'm ready now, I said.

—No, Sharon said. You're not.

Sharon was not there after school. We had walked together in the morning. I stood on a brown patch in the big green school lawn and waited. She didn't show up. The idea of trying to go home without her was scary. Something terrible might happen.

It was a warm day. I started to walk, just one little step, then another.

My mother had made me wear my warm blue jacket because the morning had been a little cool. Now I was sweating.

I started to take it off.

I heard their footsteps, their voices coming close behind me.

—Little bastard in blue.

—Little baby running scared.

—Thinks he can play dumb.

—Pretending he doesn't hear us.

I could not turn around and face them, though I knew they were right behind me. Their footsteps stopped.

—Load up.

—Big juicy one.

—Fire when ready.

The sound of street shoes stomping hard.

Loud, louder!

They were going to hit me, knock me down. I was going to be beat up. I thought of running to Sammy's Market and Liquors but knew I had no chance. Running would make it worse.

—Go, ah—!

Sploosh!

The first warm salvo hit the back of my head and ran down my neck.

I kept walking. I tried not to change speed for fear of making them angry.

—Look at him! Buck-buck-buck! Chicken-chicken!

—Lock and load loogie!

I could hear that they'd stopped and fallen back so they could come at me running again.

Sound of pounding shoes, harsh intake of break. I almost stopped to brace for impact.

The saliva hit me square in the back of my shirt. I kept walking. Wet from their spittle, I kept on walking. I was a child who let others spit on him. I was too scared to do anything about it.

Two more salvos. Their footsteps fell away as I rounded the corner past the market and headed down Blossom River Drive.

I didn't look back. If Sharon found out I was the biggest coward in school, she'd know what a terrible mistake she'd made being my friend. Why hadn't she seen it before, with the school nurse and my cowering at the fringes of the playground?

Dad's door was open for once when I got home. Like an invitation. He was sitting at his desk holding up a funny looking slip of yellow paper.

—Dad?

I slumped against the door jamb. Even with my eyes closed I could feel his attention switch to me.

—What's up, Davy?

—Dad...

—Are you crying?

I shook my head. Of course not.

—What's wrong, son?

—Some boys...

I couldn't say it.

—Davy, what did these boys do to you?

I turned around to show him my jacket that I had never managed to get off.

—What? Are you bleeding? I don't see what...

I turned and looked at my father's big unshaved face. He usually didn't shave until late in the afternoon; after a good day's work, he'd say.

—They spit on me, I said. They ran at me and spit on me. On my back. And my neck and head.

—How many of them were there?

—Three, I think.

—What did you do?

—I... Nothing. I didn't do anything. I didn't do anything at all. I just kept walking. I walked home. I walked all the way home.

Dad was nodding. He kept nodding. He nodded as if what I told him confirmed something he already knew.

—They spit on you, he said. Nice, sweet kid like you. Of course they did. And what could you do—with so many of them?

Dad stared at his wall as if trying to picture the faces of boys who would do such a thing. He shook his head.

—Fighting's no good, he said. It's stupid, takes you down to their level.

Dad looked at the piece of yellow paper in his hand.

—I'm sorry, Davy. The world is full of boys like the ones who spit on you. I wish I could lie to you and say something else, but I can't. It just isn't in me.

He waved the slip of yellow paper, then wadded it up and heaved it into the wastebasket.

—Guess you just take after me, he said.

SIX

—If he kept his distance, you'd probably be saying he was an aloof father. I mean, here I am defending the bastard, who's about as far-right Republican as you can get without falling off the edge of the world. But I have to say that witch hunts can go either way. They've got everybody looking for hobgoblins under every rock in America.

Mom and dad thought I was asleep.

I covered my head with my pillow. Sharon lived alone with her father and her brother Rodney. Both of them seemed to hate me. I was afraid of her brother Rodney who was a teenager and always looked like he wanted to beat me up. I saw Rodney and Sharon and Mr. Tammerand in their big, quiet house. Pictures came into my mind that scared me. I didn't understand the ugly inner animation my parents' words had set in motion.

I heard my mother crying.

—Oh, Graham, she's the first real friend he's ever had. It scares me so bad that he might lose her. It scares me so bad...

I knew that I would never lose Sharon. It was impossible. Mom would see to it. I went back to sleep.

On the Saturday after Thanksgiving my mom woke me up early.

—Davy? Davy, do you remember your grandfather?

My mother's eyes were red and her voice was shaky. I had heard the phone ring and mom answered it. After a while, she hung up very quietly as if she were afraid to wake someone.

—Yes, I said.

And I did, even though I'd only met him once for a few hours.

—I have to go to San Francisco, she said. I have to take the bus to San Francisco. Your father...

I followed her to the door of my father's work room. Mom tried to open it. It was locked.

—He never came to bed. I wonder if...

I watched my mother pack a small suitcase.

—You'd probably rather stay here with your father. I'll be all right. There's no need for anyone to go with me. There's no point in it, really.

She made breakfast. Our heads turned when the lock on dad's door clicked open.

—I smell something good, he said as he came out. Boy, am I hungry. What's up?

My mother, all dressed up, put my dad's plate with eggs and toast and bacon down at his place at the table.

—Regina called. It's dad. His heart again. He didn't make it this time.

My father took a step toward mom then stopped. She raised her eyebrows. Her eyes were wet but she was smiling.

—I don't suppose, she said, that you'd want to...

—

42

She held that hopeful smile.

Dad looked through the kitchen window at the falling-down garage in our backyard. Pieces of brittle wood had sprung free, spiking the air like dead weeds. The one support beam looked ready to snap.

—The work I'm doing is very difficult, he said. If I leave it now...

My mom's head dropped. She looked so pretty in her grey suit with little white lace ruffles around the neck and wrists.

—That's fine, mom said. Davy shouldn't miss any more school. It'll help a lot if you stay here with him.

—Sure, dad said.

—I'll go with you, mom, I said. I'll go with you.

She tried to smile at me. She tried so hard.

Dad made hamburgers the first night mom was gone. We sat on the front porch after dinner listening to *Suspense* on the radio. After a while he stood up and stretched his arms and said he was going for a walk.

He was gone a long time. I went back inside and drew pictures of pirates and swords and skulls and crossbones and listened to the radio.

—Davy! Wake up—guess who I just met?

Dad grabbed my shoulders and breathed into my face. His breath smelled kind of funny, but it wasn't so bad I couldn't stand it.

—Davy, what would you say if I told you that one of the greatest cowboys ever in the history of movies is living right here on our block?

I wore cowboy outfits, including hats and vests and six-shooters etched with famous cowboy signatures.

—Who, dad? Hoppy? Lash LaRue?

—No, Davy. Somebody even bigger. He made more movies than all of those others put together.

Dad looked at me to see what I thought.

I couldn't think of any cowboys I knew who'd made more movies.

—Tom Gaylord! he said. Can you believe that—Tom Gaylord right here on Blossom River Drive? Not only is he a great actor. He's got his head on straight. He's not afraid to stand up for what he believes!

I wondered why I had never heard of Tom Gaylord. Maybe there were cowboys even more famous than Hopalong Cassidy and Tom Mix and Lash LaRue.

—Listen, Davy, would you like to meet Mr. Gaylord?

I nodded.

—I make you a promise. I'll introduce you to him. Soon. Maybe tomorrow. Tomorrow's Saturday, isn't it?

Dad didn't always remember the days of the week. Sometimes he even forgot about birthdays and holidays, until mom told him.

I was going to meet the world's most famous cowboy. It seemed like a wonderful thing. How could it be anything else?

SEVEN

—Hello, little boy.

—What? Wait!

Darkness. Someone in my room. I tried to pull away.

—Ssssh! It's a game. Hello, little boy. Say *hello*.

I mouthed it. She had one hand on my chest, pushing me down; the other hand lifted to make a shape.

—See? He's the finger man. He likes you. You have to do what he says. It's Saturday and he wants to play!

Sharon's upside-down hand walked on my bed. The two fingers she used were the middle finger and the one next to the thumb.

—Watch him, silly! Just watch!

The finger man went into the air in a long effortless jump. He hung there for a second, like a cartoon character who doesn't know yet that he's supposed to fall. Then he dropped onto the bedspread and ran up the side of my stomach. I flinched.

—Ticklish? Don't worry. The finger man is going to save you from an army of monsters that's climbing onto your bed.

Raise your knee. See, he goes up-up-up this hill and—wham, slam, bash—he beats up the bad monsters and slaughters them to bits. There! They're all dead!

The fingers jumped onto my forehead and walked down my face.

They stopped on my chin.

—Finger man is a great hero. Do you like him? Huh, huh?

—I like him a lot. I know a finger man, too. See?

I turned a little on my side to free my hand from my outer space bedspread. My finger man was smaller than hers. The two climbed the bedspread hill together, bounding over the runaway asteroids and purple-ringed planets. Leaping higher and higher.

Her finger man came down and landed on mine and started kicking him.

—Hey.

Finger man turned into an octopus, all five fingers fighting. It grabbed my fingers and squeezed them.

—Want to hear a secret?

It was the finger man talking.

—Lay still. I said still.

He climbed my shoulder and went up the side of my head to my ear.

—Stop squirming! You have to hear this secret from finger man.

—Okay.

I lay still. He stepped on my ear.

—Do you like Sharon?

I nodded.

—You're supposed to say...

She paused.

—Oh well. So guess what? We got a television. Do you know what that is?

I'd seen television sets that played in the windows of

—

department stores. My face pressed to cool glass, I had strained to touch the pictures on the little screen.

—Want to come over to my house and see? Sharon said in her own voice. My dad's working a half day and he won't be home until after lunch.

—What about your brother?

I was afraid of Rodney. He was fourteen. He always glared and walked straight at me. I had to jump out of his way to keep from getting run over.

—He went downtown with his friends.

—But if my dad...

—You said he stays in his room and never opens the door.

Sharon wore her western shirt with the red and green and yellow glass beads all over it.

—Maybe you don't want to see television, she said. Maybe you want the finger man to *kill* you.

The finger man jumped and tried to get me under the covers right through my pajamas.

—No!

I jumped out of bed to avoid the finger man and got a pinch on my hip.

—OOOh. I saw something, Sharon said.

I turned my back to straighten my pajama bottoms.

—You didn't see anything, I said.

She nodded slowly, her eyes slitted. She smiled.

—Anyway! Let's go watch television.

Sharon stood in the kitchen while I dressed.

It felt funny putting on my shirt and jeans and my belt and shoes with her out there.

—Come on! Hurry up!

I closed the back screen door quietly and we raced through the icy wind and up her front porch. Her house was warm inside.

—

—See?

The television was placed on a little metal table with legs crossed under it and locked solid. The screen seemed to be looking at me. Her house was quiet in a different way than our house was.

—Watch!

Sharon turned a knob. The square-faced screen got grey, clouded up like something was wrong. Then I heard voices. Then there were people sitting in a row.

—While the senator now suggests he can prove...

—Boring stuff. Watch this.

Sharon turned another knob. Trees blowing in the wind. A man talking. Someone throwing a big black ball down a track.

—There! Look. Cartoons.

I knew these characters. The one with the little head under a sailor cap and crazy bulging muscles. The skinny girl with black pigtails who looked like she would bend in two. Sharon and I watched up close, lying on our stomachs with our heads propped up in our hands. It was just like the movies, except right in front of you so that somehow it seemed like it was part of your life instead of something you only visited.

Sharon bumped me.

—Want to play with finger man?

I was perfectly happy being there with her watching the picture box that had suddenly come into her living room. I didn't want to change anything.

I shook my head.

Sharon pulled away.

—You don't want to play finger man?

I shrugged.

Was Sharon upset? I hardly noticed when she left.

The cartoons were over, but now there was a woman who

ducked down behind a box or sometimes stood up over it. She had two friends, a puppet dragon and a puppet bear.

The dragon had crooked teeth that didn't seem like they could bite anything. His eyes were crossed and he rested his head on the box.

—Oh, it's rainy outside today. Woe is me. I hate rain. It makes me feel gloomy. I'm going to be in a real bad mood, right now!

The bear was much smaller, but he bounced in and climbed over the dragon.

—Arise, Draggy! There's so many fun things to do inside when it's raining outdoors!

—Oh, you always say that. Why can't you let me be gloomy and sad for once? I don't think it's very nice that we have to be happy all the time.

The front door opened and Rodney came in. He stopped where he stood when he saw me lying on the floor in front of the new television set. I started to get up to get out of his way.

—Sharon said I could...

He shrugged and left the room. The bear and the dragon were mad at each other. They had their hands folded and stood far away from each other on different sides of the box.

Things were so bad the nice lady had to come to talk to them.

—What's the matter, Browny? she said.

—Gloomy Draggy's at it again, he said.

The nice lady's lips moved a little when Browny spoke.

Rodney came back into the room. I got ready to get out of the way. But he sat on the small sofa Sharon called a love seat. I thought he'd be looking at me in a mean way, but he seemed to be watching the show. This surprised me because he said he hated *little kid stuff*.

—You too, Draggy, the lady said. You both have to learn to see the other one's point of view. Draggy, do you know what that's called?

The dragon looked more unhappy than ever. He shook his head slowly to say that he didn't know what it was called. It was kind of funny and sad at the same time.

—When you and Browny talk things through and work out your problems, that's called *compromise*. Every friendship needs at least a little bit of it and everybody...

Rodney slid down to the floor. I thought he was going to hit me. Or shove me out of the way. But he didn't. He sat there and put his head in his hands the way I had mine. He was watching the show!

Rodney had big shoulders and muscles that showed when his white T-shirt bunched up, like now. He had a little smell of sweat or something else, but I didn't mind because he was being nice. It was amazing for him to sit close to me.

Rodney rose up on one elbow. He seemed smaller than he ever had, as if he'd become a little kid so that we could enjoy television together. I turned toward him a little and started to smile.

—What's your name again? Rodney said.

The way he spoke quietly and not fast and angry made me see that he wanted to be my friend.

I said my name.

His mouth and eyebrows scrunched up in a funny way and he came close as if he wanted to whisper a secret.

—Davy? he said

I nodded. Yes, he had it right. That was my name.

His face came close to mine. He looked toward the ceiling.

—Would you suck my dickie if I washed it?

My face got hot. I pulled away from him. At first I didn't understand. Then I did.

I couldn't look at him. I shook my head.

I stared at the Tammerand's television as printed words came on the screen saying who was what and who did what on the puppet show.

I felt sick. I knew I wasn't going to throw up, but I wished I could stop feeling what I was feeling and seeing in my mind what I was seeing.

Rodney was gone before I noticed that he'd gotten up.

Another program came on, but I didn't know anything about it. Sharon came back into the room and dropped down beside me. It was a long time before we spoke.

—Are you surprised I get to play with you again?

—I guess.

—We can't ever play that game again, Dad says. Dad says it was a bad game. Do you think it was bad?

—I don't know, I said.

—Maybe we can play it in a different way, she said.

—Sure. Maybe.

—You'd better go. Dad'll be home soon.

—Rodney was here.

—I saw him, she said.

I went back to my house and didn't see my father. The door of his room was closed. I heard the radio playing in there. The master bedroom door was open. My mother was on the bed. Every day I had waited for her to come back home and now here she was. She had the same pretty suit on that she wore when she left to go to see her father get buried. Did she wear it the whole time she was gone? Her red scarf was bunched up around her neck like it was hurting her throat. The suitcase with the rest of her clothes and stuff was beside her on the bed.

I sat down on the other side of her, away from the suitcase. She raised her head a little.

—Hi, honey. Were you next door playing with Sharon?

■

51

I thought about it.

—Yes, I said.

—That's nice.

—Mom?

—Yes, honey?

—Mom, I just...

—What?

She tried to raise up but she didn't seem to be able to.

—I'm sorry, Davy. I have a terrible headache. The doctor had a new name for it, but I can't remember the word. What did you want to tell me?

—Mom...

I had to say it. I had to.

—Mom, I'm sorry. I'm sorry about your father, your dad.

—Oh, honey.

—I'm sorry grandpa died. I'm sorry. I'm sorry. I'm sorry!

I hugged her really hard, almost as if I was angry at her, almost as if I was so angry I'd never let go of her.

—It's okay, honey, she said. It's alright. It's alright.

She hugged me, too. And the strength in her arms surprised me. I could feel her crying. But I was crying harder and I wasn't sure why.

—

EIGHT

—My dad says he's a commonist and that it's funny suspicious your dad hanging around with him all the time. My dad says he drinks. A lot.

It seemed so important to understand these hard adult words that were in the air around us.

—But he's a famous cowboy, I said. The most famous in all the world.

—Says who?

—Well, he is. Besides, I think that maybe your brother is a commonist, too.

—Rodney? That's stupid. He's not old enough to be one.

I put my face against Sharon's face the way we did when we made a real pledge.

—I'm pretty sure, I said.

Sharon shifted her legs around in the gravel behind our garage. It was our new hiding place. Her dad said to never play here because it was filthy. But Sharon was good at making her

-

dress look clean again even after we played in twigs and dirt and gravel.

Her eyes narrowed. She hit her hand into her fist.

—We'll have to spy on *all* of them.

—Really?

Sharon raised her head. She looked up past the telephone poles and wires into the bright blue sky.

—Don't you see? she said. It's part of the big plan. That's why they won't let us play that other game that we won't even say the name of because it's so bad. We were wrong, Davy!

—I don't get it, I said.

—We were wrong thinking that the electric chair—whoops!—that bad thing we don't talk about was the most dangerous and terrible and awful of all! It's this man pretending to be a famous cowboy and your father—and maybe my brother, too! We have to find out who's really bad and stop him before he does something really terrible.

One night mom grabbed dad's hand as he was tried to get up from dinner.

—Honey, are you sure you're getting enough work done? We've been putting off vacations and family visits so you could finish your writing. Are you sure—

—No one knows but me, dad said. No one knows but the artist.

Mom rolled a flowered hot pad and started to hold it up to the kitchen light like she was going to use it as a telescope.

—Do you have to go down to Tom's every night? she said. Maybe if you stayed and did some writing—

—I'm tired at night. I need to get out.

—Well, maybe you and I could...

—Tom's had a hard time since his wife left. Besides, I like talking to him.

—Well, why don't you have him come down here sometimes?

—Maybe I will, dad said.

Two days later it was mom's birthday. Dad and I surprised her with a chocolate cake we got at John's Gourmet Bakery on Sycamore Street. It had candles and a pretty yellow candy rose in the middle and green sugar leaves.

We had just finished singing Happy Birthday to her, just dad and me. And mom was wiping her eyes with her apron.

—All right, Kay. It's time to make a wish!

—GR-RAY! someone yelled in through our screen door. GR-RAY!

The doorbell rang.

There was a loud knock on the screen door and almost at the same time it flew open.

A wide man came in and stood facing me, hands on his hips. He had the darkest, blackest hair I had ever seen, and a mustache and a little bunch of hair on his chin that was black too. His eyebrows, which were very bushy and wild, were white. How was that possible?

—GR-RAY, boy—what have we here?

The wide man seemed to be challenging us right in our own house. Like someone in a movie.

—Little family affair, huh? Looks like someone's celebrating themselves some sort of milestone.

Mom was poised over the cake. Her candles were still burning.

Dad bumped his knee jumping up from the table.

—Kay, Davy—my friend, the greatest cowboy actor of all time, Tom Gaylord.

■

Mr. Gaylord seemed to think about my dad's words for a minute before he looked at us again.

He put his arm around my dad's shoulders. Dad was taller, by quite a bit. Mr. Gaylord was shorter than any of the cowboys I'd seen.

—Hi, family, he said. Hope you folks 'ppreciate this man you got yourselves here. Know how rare it is, having a real man in your house and holding up your household?

He stared at me and then at my mom. He had to stand almost on his tiptoes to keep his big arm around dad's shoulder.

—I'll say the word emasculatin' for the sake of this young boy here, though I 'spect he knows the genuine words. Emasculation is the name of the game the money boys play— telling you how to act and who to be friends with and what you can join and what you can't. All the new so-called cow-boys come pre-sissified so the corporate butchers don't have to cut nothin' off or modify a damn thing to get them to be and say and act just how they want.

—Tom...

My dad and Mr. Gaylord rocked back and forth. It looked like they were dancing. But dad was slipping away from Mr. Gaylord's arm.

—What you got here as a daddy and a husband is a *man*— a genius, if you ask me. Yes, I've read his fine words. Heard 'em on the airways, too. And the *only* reason he ain't rich and famous right this second is that he won't drop his pants and put the pair of 'em right there on the chopping—

—Tom! You came just in time to see my wife blow out her candles and have some birthday cake with us! Why don't you sit down and—

—Cake?

Mr. Gaylord squinted at the white wheel with the yellow rose and candles.

—That? That's poison. Processed sugar's *pure poison,* plain and simple. Might as well be putting grounded up glass in your stomach and churning it 'round a bit.

Mr. Gaylord struggled to keep his short arm around my dad's shoulders as they swayed. My dad smiled extra big the way he did when he wanted to impress someone with something smart.

—Tom's Hollywood's only honest man, he said to mom and me. Do you know why they fired him from his last movie? He insisted on having a Negro man ride a horse and play a serious part instead of just being a cook or flunky—

—Black, brown, yellow, red, all're equal under the skin. I've befriended 'em all if they were men, balled 'em if they were women.

—Tom?

My dad fought his arm around behind Mr. Gaylord's and they wrestled for whose arm was on top of the other's shoulder.

—Tom? Buddy? Maybe tonight's not the night for this.

Mr. Gaylord threw off my dad's arm and pulled away toward the door.

—Think I'm not good enough? he said. Think I'm just an a god damn has-been? Washed-up old drunk? You told 'em 'bout me? 'Bout what I can do for you? Our big plans?

Dad took Mr. Gaylord aside and whispered to him. Mr. Gaylord hollered right in dad's face, but after dad talked some more he seemed to calm down. They pulled apart and then, almost bashfully, shook each other's hand.

—I'll be down to see you in a bit, Tom. Honey, let's cut the cake and finish up here. Mr. Gaylord and I have a few things to discuss before I hit the sack tonight.

Dad helped with the dishes, then headed down the street. I was standing just behind mom as she watched dad through the front window.

■

—How does he find these crazy men? How does he do it, no matter where we move? How does he find them?

I shuffled my feet and she saw me.

—Oh, honey, I didn't mean for you to hear me.

Mom knelt down in front of me.

—I didn't really mean what I just said. Your father is a wonderful man who believes in wonderful, important things.

She studied my face to see if I understood.

—He's brave to stand up for what he believes in. Except sometimes I wish he...

Mom shook her head with her eyes closed.

—No, it's me, she said. I wish I wasn't such a scaredy-cat. I wish my mind didn't always make me worry that something bad was going to happen. Know what, honey?

In that moment I would have done or said anything to make her happy.

—What, mom?

—I'm glad that you take after your father. I can see it more and more, all the time.

For Christmas I got a Head Inspector Investigating Kit. It had a magnifying glass, paper and ink for fingerprints, powder for footprints, handcuffs, a badge, and a little book on how to break codes and create your own secret code, and another pocket-sized book on how to catch crooks. Like me, Sharon had put her best present at the top of her list and left the rest blank. Her Buster-You're-Under-Arrest Official Crime Station included pads with all the information to book criminals. Spaces were included for their names, ages, addresses, height, weight, and occupation. There was space for writing down all their *activities*, especially their crimes. She also had a magnifying glass.

But inside the orange and black box was a nightstick for stopping crooks and burglars and a chief-of-police hat.

We started right away writing down all the vital information about Mr. Gaylord and my dad and Rodney. It amazed us how quickly everything took shape on the booking sheet.

We got my dad's fingerprints when I told him it was a game. He smiled and told me how *clever* I was. I felt bad for tricking him. Sharon got Rodney's fingerprints off a bottle of beer he sneaked into his room out of the refrigerator. We weren't sure how we were going to get Mr. Gaylord's prints, but we knew we had to if we wanted to solve this case.

My mother's headaches were worse. She told me in the nicest way to behave (which she said I always did anyway) and apologized over and over for asking me to look after myself. I seemed to have a lot more time to myself. Sharon and I spent every spare moment we could looking through Mr. Gaylord's window, spying on him and my dad.

NINE

—Does your mother ever scream?

Summer came and school was over.

—What?

We were in our most secret place about three blocks past the playground of the school. It was near the dry river that people called an arroyo. Sharon and I called it a canyon. It had ancient oak and eucalyptus trees growing all the way up to the top so that most places you couldn't see down to the bottom. Not unless you climbed out into the trees.

—Scream? I said. You mean like getting hurt?

Sharon shook her head. We were alone, as far as we knew, kneeling on the ground between two oak trees. She put her mouth close to my ear.

—Before my mother went away, sometimes she'd go into the bedroom with my father and lock the door. You know?

She seemed to be asking if I believed this could happen. I nodded. I believed it.

—I'd listen and look in through the keyhole. They'd get on

the bed. I could only see the end of the bed. After some other noises, she'd scream sometimes, like oooohhhhh-ahhhh-oooohhh.

—Really? I said.

—And since she's been gone, my father... Davy, I hate him sometimes. But I want to scream like that. I want to learn how to scream like that.

She looked at me so intently, not blinking at all.

—Okay, I said.

—It has to start with taking off your clothes. Let's take off our clothes. Then maybe if we lie down I can start screaming.

I thought of the beautiful woman who screamed in the comic book. How her long pretty black hair caught on fire and she ran screaming through her house. Her house was so expensive and large and spacious that she ran through it without ever reaching the end. Only one other comic book scared me that bad.

—Did you hear that? I said.

—What?

—Listen!

Sharon turned to listen. I bent and grabbed a rock. I threw it toward the middle of the canyon where there were lots of trees growing up from the bottom. There was the sound of rustling through the big dry live oaks and then shuffling and struggling through brush and against big rocks and river gravel.

—A monster! I said. Can't you hear it?

Sharon had her hand on her throat. What if she pulled up her dress?

—I did hear something, she said.

I turned away. I folded my arms.

—I'm not sure, I said. Maybe there wasn't anything.

—There was, she said. There was. Listen.

■

I kept my back turned. I heard Sharon's dress rustle as if she had bent down and then came up again real fast.

Seconds later, I heard it. Something falling, slouching, lumbering through the brush, through the big silent dry trees.

—I heard it!

—He lives in the canyon, Sharon said.

—No one's ever seen him, I said.

—He kills for his food.

—He kills anything he can get.

—If he has to, he climbs up and comes out.

We listened to our own words and they silenced us. We walked to the edge of the canyon. A great stillness came up all the way from the bottom. A bird cried in the highest branches of a tree that grew up from down inside and arched high over our heads. The bird flew away as if it had startled itself with its own cry.

—He knows we're here.

—He's listening to us now.

—He knows something about us.

—He knows...our names.

—Names don't mean anything to him, Sharon said. He knows where things are. He knows paths and underground tunnels. And how to get around without being seen. He knows how to find us.

—He knows where we live.

—No matter where we go in the world, no matter how far away we are, he knows how to find us and how to get us.

—He knows *everything*. He—

Sharon shook her head. Neither of us took our eyes off the canyon.

—He's blind. He can only find what he can smell—

—And hear.

—And taste and lick and rub against.

—

—He's blind and mean and terrible.

—But he wants something. He wants something special and important. And if we can find out what that is, maybe we can stop him from killing more people.

—He's killed before, I said. He'll kill again. But first we have to find him. We have to find out where he is.

Sharon turned from the cliff, shaking her head as if this were an impossible puzzle. Something we could never hope to answer.

I bent to pick up a small red rock. It was so pretty and smooth and round in my hand that I knew I had to throw it quickly or it would end up at the bottom of my left pocket. My right pocket had a hole in it and I only put things there that I didn't want to keep.

A noise came out of the canyon. It sounded like something stumbled, righted itself, jumped, tumbled, then came to rest with two strong stomps at the very bottom.

—Oh!

Sharon spun around and grabbed my arm.

—He heard us, she said. He knows we know. He knows about—us.

I nodded, feeling my throat tighten.

—He knows how special we are, you and me. He knows there aren't another two like us in the world. We aren't afraid to find out things. And when we find them out, nobody can stop us.

She grabbed my arm harder. It almost hurt, but I was glad.

—Davy, let's let him know we're brave. He thinks we're not. Let's let him know he's wrong.

—Okay. How? I don't want to go down there. He runs so fast that—

—We can't go down there. It's instant death. But we're braver than he thinks and we've got to show him. We've got to show him or he'll come after us. Tonight. In our beds. While we're sleeping. No, what we've got to do is scream. Think you can do it?

Sharon had her hands on my shoulders. She looked me straight in the eye until I nodded *yes*, I could.

We turned to face the canyon. It was bigger, so much bigger than I'd ever noticed. We stepped to the very edge.

We looked at each other. We opened our mouths.

We screamed.

Our voices went down into the canyon. There was a kind of echo. Then a hidden bird flew up and there was a shifting sound, a stirring like something waking up and stumbling.

I turned my head and the amazingly lifelike noises came out of the canyon. Even though I threw rocks into the arroyo and those rocks made sounds, it was hard for me to believe that there wasn't something actually down there. The sounds were real. Even if we made them, they were real. And there was something more there, more than the sounds any spinning stone could make in brush and dirt.

—AEIII-eeeee! AHHH-AAHHH!

The screams were ours. And we listened after screaming for answers from down inside.

Once we heard what sounded like a long drawn-out laugh, sort of high, but also scary. It definitely came from down at the bottom. He was mocking us. He was mocking us for playing there at his serious place where he lived.

—He's so old, Sharon said.

—He's older than anybody else.

—He wants us to know he's there, she said.

By now, I was quite sure that she was right about that.

—Why?

—Because he knows. He knows other people see us as kids. He knows that no one will believe us.

-

65

She turned. I found a good round clod of dirt and threw it as far as I could. There was hardly a sound.

Sharon looked at me as if I'd done something bad.

—Stand over there, she said. Leave it to me to see if he's still there.

Her dress whispered, thrashed.

I turned.

We listened.

Nothing.

—Nothing.

—Let's get out of here before he comes back.

We headed off.

A flat stone caught my eye. I dropped to tie my shoelace. Sharon walked ahead.

When I stood up, Sharon turned.

And together we heard it, as if some great animal, or man-beast, moved again, safe in the knowledge that we were finally leaving. So safe he was ready to laugh that awful laugh.

—Let's go.

—Yes.

Neither of us looked behind us. We knew the thing in the canyon would be there when we came back.

The two glowing points moved a little in the darkness. Sometimes they'd swoop and glide, then go back to not moving again. We'd waited until dark so that we wouldn't be seen crouching outside Mr. Gaylord's window spying on him and my dad. We'd squeezed ourselves between the low window and the rose bushes. The ground under the rose bushes was cracked and hard. The rose thorns were long and sharp and really hurt if they got into you.

We had water glasses pressed against the window with the

open ends to our ears like the detective book said to do. The window was open and we could hear at least as much through the opening as we could through the glass.

—See, there? That's the double. *Double!* Think his shoulders look broad as mine? And look at that fat, sloppy butt on him! Now, watch this scene where he jumps off the horse to catch the run away wagon.

—They're smoking!

—SSSh! I said.

I could see a corner of the screen. I could also see the small movie projector. It was darker than anything else in the room. The block of machinery had spinning hoops of film at both ends. Light shot across the smoky air onto the little white screen. Three cowboys at a waterhole crouched behind some rocks and sagebrush.

—There—you always know when it's me! See how I swing down from the wagon? Make it look easy, don't I?

—Absolutely, my dad said in the dark. Smooth!

The movie's sound was turned down so low you could hardly hear it. You couldn't tell if there was any music.

—I had to convince Parker to let me do that one. He talked insurance and contracts and not putting a guy out of a job. I says I don't put nobody out of a job if they know how to do their damn job. Didn't I make the studio hire *him* even though he was a champion juicer? Knew he could do the job, that's all.

—Is that you, Tom? In this fight sequence here?

—Now you tell me. What d'ya see?

—Well...

The cowboy in the checkered shirt was the hero. If it was supposed to be Mr. Gaylord, it was him when he was very young. The three men from the waterhole had the drop on him, but he pushed one into the other. Then he grabbed the nearest one and started punching him. His back was to the camera.

—

—Seems pretty graceful, my dad said. I mean, coordinated and natural.

—Yeah? Watch the punches. Call that close? Got to be so close that you think it's landed. So close that sometimes you do connect and knock some fool silly. That look close to you, Graham?

—Well...no. Not really. No, no. That's definitely not you. That's definitely your double. He doesn't have your...timing or your sense of—

—Did you hear something?

—No. I see what you mean. The sound effects of knuckles striking skin don't coincide—

—Outside. Ah, forget it. Kids, probably. I attract 'em like flies. So what about it, Gray? When're you going to start writing that script for me? Catch that light, would you? Gonna put on one more reel. One last history lesson for tonight.

—Well, dad said, his voice kind of quiet. I've got some ideas. It's a big change for me, Tom. In radio, the words make pictures. With movies, words seem like—

—You starting to get the feel for who Tom Gaylord is? You see what Hollywood lost themselves when they let Tom Gaylord get away?

Sharon and I cupped our water glasses to our chests and hugged ourselves. We had almost been caught. I could hear better now.

—Hollywood lost a living legend when it lost you, Tom.

—Here, let me fill that up for you. So, what's your approach? How are you going to start the thing?

—Well...

I could hear my dad exhaling cigar smoke. The rich plumes of tobacco floated out the window and down to Sharon and me. It seemed like a gift, the smell and texture of my father's smoke.

I licked the air. I licked my chin and lip and thought I could taste tobacco leaves.

—In the opening, I see you as a young guy just arrived in Hollywood. Your luggage will have a sticker from Waukegan so that we get your hometown in there. Soon as you arrive at the first studio, you see this beautiful Mexican girl standing on the street in tears. You go up to her and offer your handkerchief and ask—

—No, no, no, no! Starts in Illinois. I'm a little kid. Reading an old penny dreadful. Camera comes in close. I'm talking to myself, thinking aloud. *Someday,* I say. *Someday, I'm going to have adventures like that. And everybody'll see me save the world.*

—And you did, as an actor, an artist.

—Sure I did. That's what you've got to put in this picture we're making. Get the lights, will you? This next one'll give you some fuel for that persnickety pen of yours.

Showdown at Sun Mesa. Starring Tom Gaylord and Evelyn Fritch. With Paul Haverley and Deforest Roadcape.

—Watch this opening real careful. We were out in the back lot. Been raining something fierce. I had to do this bareback thing and keep my costume dry. Got to shape the lasso while trying to keep my horse on her feet. Plus I got a god damn fascist for a director who's already talking about names on some list.

—Hard to imagine, my dad said. You make it all look so effortless.

I had a cramp in my foot and shifted a little. A rose thorn went right into my neck. I put my finger in my mouth and bit down so I wouldn't make a sound.

Sharon and I gathered our equipment and crept out of the bushes. We hopped onto the sidewalk and stood still as if we'd been there all the time.

—Whew! I said. Close call!

Sharon looked at me so hard that I had to look to see what she was looking at.

—Your dad, she said. Your dad is really, really, really in bad trouble. Did you hear what they're plotting to do?

—What?

—They're plotting to make commonist movies. If we can't think of a way to save him soon, it's going to be the end for him.

I saw that Sharon was right. She was always right.

TEN

I lost Sharon's criminal record book two days later and she was mad at me. Then we found it and both got bored.

I had some lunch and rubbed my mom's back a while. Her headaches were worse. Her sewing had really piled up. Mom was mad at herself and apologized for leaving me alone so much. I think my dad was in his room. The door was closed.

There was nothing to do. I thought that it was the first time I'd felt that way since I met Sharon.

She was out in our backyard where the driveway ended near the back fence where there were so many weeds. She had her side to me so that I didn't know if she saw me or not while she was doing it.

Where had Sharon seen such a thing? I had seen girls do cheers and jumping at games when we walked past the junior high school where we'd be going soon. But I had never seen what she did then. And I had never seen Sharon try anything like it before. I didn't know she was so agile.

She did it fast with one easy movement. Her hands went

down, her feet went up. She was wearing her gingham dress with the colorful pattern.

Her bare legs raised in the air like arms. I had never seen anything like her two legs. They were small at the ankle and then shaped like there was something strong and sleek and lean inside, which I knew was muscle.

She didn't move. She stayed like that. Her legs in the air, her hands pressed against the gravel ground.

Seeing her made me want something. I wanted to do something to her. Her body was so flexible and perfect that I wanted to take her and snap her in two or grab both her hands and crack her in the air and make her pop like a whip.

My friend, my playmate.

It was good, how I felt, and I did not want to make it go away. But I knew it was something I had to keep to myself.

My dad had told my mom to stop bathing me several years before. He said I was more than old enough to wash myself. I liked her to bathe me because I liked to watch the lightbulb over the tub reflected in the water. I never got tired of watching the bobbing light that became so many people and faces, heroes and ships and shapes from the past and the future. All the shapes were different and surprising, their variety never-ending.

I hadn't felt anything like this since then. But this was stronger, a thousand times stronger.

My friend, my only playmate.

Maybe it was wrong, but I didn't really think it was.

I went back into the house so that I didn't have to talk to Sharon or look her in the face. I never saw her finish her handstand.

—The forces of our world do not allow for this so-called craft of yours, Regart.

—But without my work on the solar wings, the men of Lecanorga cannot safely fly beyond the atmosphere!

—Your work! Hah! Your work is mere decoration! No more, no less.

They hadn't broadcast any of dad's stories in almost six months. Mom told me this was an old one he'd sold back when we still lived in Belvedere, a place I was starting to have trouble remembering.

—See, Your Excellency? The pigment I graze against the outer layer of parchment on the wings is almost weightless. But the shapes it forms, the truths about the unity and oneness of our people, these are what lend that last iota of lift, just enough to allow the wings to break through the restraining atmosphere.

I had not told Sharon about tonight's program.

But here she was. I wouldn't look at her. But she was all I could think about or see in my mind. Her legs had caught the afternoon light and they were round, so amazingly round. And everything else, the gravel, the houses, the sky, was grey and bare. How could anything in this world be so beautiful? I didn't know that it could grab you in the stomach and twist so that you wanted to yell.

Her face was always in front of me now. I always thought of her face as round. It got long when she was mad or excited about something. But now I saw that her face wasn't round at all. Her forehead curved in a way that made me want to put my fingers there and feel how it was shaped. Her cheeks looked as strong and firm as all the rest of her, but now I pictured them in the times we were together and saw them to be like clay we molded when we were little. Her cheeks could be pinched and squeezed and grabbed and held out from her face. I knew that now. Her lips were maneuverable too. All the words they had said to me. Her lips were mine, in a way, because so many of

—

73

the words that came out of them came out to me. Were said to me. I never thought of her lips as more than skin on her mouth that moved when she talked or made a pouting look. But now they seemed like buildings, maybe those tubes that made up the space station model we'd assembled last winter. They could be occupied by maybe lots of people, with all sorts of amazing unseen activities going on inside.

—They're falling! The men of Lecanorga are falling from the sky! They are dying! They are dying! All our best and bravest citizens are smashing their bodies on the ground!

Her eyes were the end or the center of everything. I had looked at them a million times. I had even looked into them trying to find certain things. Was she mad at me? Would today be a good day?

But I had never looked into them only to look into them. To look into her. Now, her face was there, all of it. But I saw nothing but her eyes. Hazel. Or brown, with green. And through them I could look into Sharon. It was all I ever wanted to do. What else could there ever be in the world to do?

—The wax, the wax fashioned by the Softworkers' Guild! The wax must have melted!

—No, look here at Hranthdon. His wings are intact. The wax has held. Only—

—Everything is the same. Nothing has been changed. These men could not have fallen.

—Are you sure, Excellency? Are you positive that everything is the same?

—Well...

—Everything?

—Everything except those ludicrous scratches that fool Regart appended after all the real work was done.

—Yes, his *decorations*. His adornments. And how lovingly he applied them! Once and forever, when the men of Lecanorga flew on wings of gossamer light, they did not fall. And Lecanorga ruled the skies and all the Tangent Worlds. Now, doomed. Doomed! Guards, arrest His Excellency! Find the man Regart and bring him to me now.

—It is too late, Superintendent Marcus. He was last seen at the walls near the Garden of Alcambertus assembling and donning the last set of wings he was permitted to adorn. He was here and then—

One step. One step into those eyes and I would be lost forever.

—I couldn't sleep last night, Sharon said.

We were on the back porch. We'd helped my mom fold some clothes fresh off the line. We were just sitting there listening to the cicadas being crybabies because of the heat.

—Why couldn't you? I said.

—Have you ever thought—?

—What?

—Never mind.

—What?

—It's just real stupid. Just real terrible and stupid.

She closed her eyes and shook her head as if she might start crying. She never cried.

—What, Sharon?

—Remember the game we used to play last year when I first met you?

—Yes.

—When we were playing, did you ever think about it? Ever. Really, actually think about it?

—Think about what?

—Last night I was lying in bed. That dog that got hit by the car yesterday..?

—

I hadn't seen the dog hit, but I came out of the house and saw it lying on Sharon's lawn like it was tired. I couldn't see anything wrong with it. It wasn't moving. A man from across the street kneeled down next to the dog. The dog was very still even when he touched it. The man, who was young and handsome, asked for a mirror and someone brought him one. He took the mirror in his hand and put it close to the dog's face, up against the dog's nose. He examined the small mirror and then rubbed it against his sleeve and put it into the dog's face again. I whispered to ask what he was doing. *Trying to see if he's breathing,* he said. I saw Sharon looking over my shoulder. The handsome young man took a handkerchief out of his pocket and covered the dog's face. It was a big dog and its black and brown ears stuck out from the little white handkerchief. I had watched Sharon go back into her house without saying anything.

Sharon looked at me in a way she never had before. It was something in her face I had never seen.

—Have you ever thought that one day you won't be alive any more?

I couldn't answer right away. The words she said could have been my words. I felt my chest open up and something flooded out.

—One night, I said. I couldn't sleep. I thought that someday I would die. A day like this. Today. Or any day.

Sharon nodded. She watched me so close and listened so hard I thought she might grab me.

—A day would come and I would be dead like I had never lived at all. And that would be forever.

—Forever, she said.

We dropped our heads.

—It can't be true, she said.

—It can't be.

—But it is.

76

—Yeah, I said. Yeah, it is.

—You didn't sleep the whole night? I mean the night it happened to you. The night you knew it?

—I couldn't sleep the whole night, I said. It was too awful. It was something so awful that it made everything else...

—It's like we're dead already. Because we know it. Does anyone else know it?

I shook my head.

—They can't. If they did, how would they live? How could they?

—How could they, she said. I was awake and I was so scared I cried. I am going to be dead. Someday I am going to be dead. Like that dog. Like grandma. Someday something will happen and I won't be alive and I won't ever be alive again. Ever. Forever and forever.

—I think that they think they know it, I said. I think that they think they know it's going to happen. They think about it maybe a little, but they don't... They don't really know it like...

I almost said *like I do.*

—Like we do.

—I'm never going to sleep again, Sharon said. I'm never going to sleep.

—It doesn't work, I said. I've tried. You have to sleep sometime.

—Oh.

—But that doesn't mean you and I can't...

—Davy, let's go to the canyon and scream and...

Sharon put her face in her elbow where the sleeve of her blouse ended.

—Let's go to the canyon and see if he's there. Okay?

—We'll scream at that old man or whatever he is.

—And we'll tell him he's going to die.

—Right! We'll tell him so he'll know.

-

—That'll fix him.

—Let's go right now, she said.

—Sure, I said. Right now.

And we did. Oh, my, did we! We yelled down into that canyon all afternoon until we were hoarse and our voices were less than whispers. We had to make sure. The thing down there really needed to know the most horrible thing in the world that no one had dared to tell it before.

ELEVEN

I thought mom and the tall woman looked funny standing up in our dining room. People always sat down in there. But mom and the woman had cups of tea in their hands and mom had put a little dish of sugar cookies on the table. They were standing within arm's reach of the dish and holding their tea cups and talking quietly.

I didn't remember the woman until my mom introduced her as my Aunt Regina.

—Quiet, aren't you? said Aunt Regina.

She wasn't really fat, but she was a big woman with big shoulders and arms. She wore earrings that were like circus hoops and a scarf around her neck. She made our house seem small by being in it.

—Davy, honey? Why don't you and Sharon go and play? Davy has the most wonderful friend. Don't you, honey? You should see them, Regina. Inseparable. Better than brother and sister—they never fight. They're just perfect little people.

—Hmmm, said Aunt Regina.

-

I went to my room. It seemed too complicated to explain to them that Sharon had gone to court with her father. It had something to do with her mother not being in the house with them. Sharon said her dad was angry. She always tried to keep him from getting too mad. She tried to stop it before it happened, if she could. Bad things happened when he got mad. So today she'd gone with him to court without his having to ask twice, even though she didn't really want to.

I closed my door, but not all the way.

Mom and Aunt Regina were quiet for a moment, as if they were listening to me.

Someone made a heavy sigh.

—I can't stand it, Aunt Regina said. I just can't stand it.

—I know it's hard, my mom said. It's real hard on all of us. It was bad enough with dad.

—Bad? It almost killed me, Kay.

The big woman took one step closer to my mother.

—I was there around the clock, night and day. To see that happen to anyone is dreadful enough, but to see if happen to the man who held you and rocked you and played softball with you and waited up for you when you started dating and gave you away at the altar...

There were whispered words I couldn't hear.

—But now, with this... I don't think I can take it, Kay. I don't think I can.

—Oh, Reggie. You're always so strong and wonderful! I don't know what the rest of us would do without you.

—No. I think what is going to happen is that one day I will simply not be able to do it for one more second, one single instant. And that will be it. They'll put me away someplace. And that will be the end of that. The end of Regina Templeton Levy. And no bright lights, and no marquee.

—Reg, please.

—

—No, listen to me, Kay. For once, listen—without trying to console me or explain or rationalize or apologize or whatever it is you always do. You're going to have to help this time. You're going to have to come up and help me with her. I just can't do the round-the-clock number again, Kay.

I peeked out the crack to see Aunt Regina take a cookie.

—Well, with Davy home and Graham...

—You said it! Davy and Graham. Kay has two children. One of them a bit overgrown—and certainly not as responsible as the littler one. In fact, how long has it been since the shiftless son of a so-and-so put so much as a loaf of bread on this table?

I couldn't make out the words my mother mumbled. Then she raised her head to look at Aunt Regina.

—Graham works very hard at his writing. They did one of his stories on NBC just last week. He does what he believes in. And I believe in it, too, Reggie.

—Well, you'd better believe your mother is dying. I could never quite convince you about dad. Not until it was too late to do anything, that is.

—Oh..!

Mom cried out like she'd been hit. I looked. She was holding her hands to her face.

She took away her hands and walked right to the big corner window and then back to Aunt Regina.

—I guess you're right, mom said. I guess you're right. I'll do my best, Regina. I can't promise to be there every single second the way you were with dad, but...

—God, I'm not asking that! Anything you can spare, Kay. A few precious minutes out of your precious life with your precious writer husband and your precious perfect little...

I put my 3-d viewer to my eyes. The picture of the beautiful woman water-skiing from the Travel Adventure series clicked into place. It was one I usually skipped. The woman had brown hair in a nice neat permanent on her head. Water sprayed up around her. She held onto the rope that was attached to the boat with one hand and smiled as if she was very happy and very nice and loved the person she smiled at. The water she skimmed over looked cold and ugly. I feared for her. I feared for what would happen if her fingers slipped and she let go. She would be down inside that horrible deep water. Down inside and under. She could never survive. Never. And yet she kept smiling. She kept holding on and smiling.

I could not click away to the next picture.

It had been a nice, sunny morning, but Sharon and I ran out of things to do. It was too hot outside, but inside it was dark and boring and a very bad sort of gloomy.

—I heard my brother talking to his stupid friend, Sharon said. They're going out to the park to meet some older guy. Want to follow them? You know, *trail* them?

Our file on Rodney included his beer bottle fingerprints, his name, address, and phone number. We had nothing yet to tie him to my dad and Mr. Gaylord.

We waited under the steps of Sharon's front porch. Rodney's quick clomping boots were big and dirty. The shoestrings were laced so tight his foot looked like a piece of meat tied up by the butcher. We watched boots turn into legs and then a whole body that went out onto the sidewalk and turned right.

—Sssh!

I was still frightened of Rodney. But I tried to keep my voice from sounding like I was begging.

—Stay out of sight! Stay out of sight!

Rodney met up with two other older boys at the park.

—Did you find her?

—Yeah, said a boy with blonde hair and big red marks on his face. She's over there in the bushes.

—I got a good supply of rocks, said the other boy.

He was very skinny. Even with his T-shirt tucked into his blue jeans there was way too much room for his waist to move around in.

Rodney and the other two loaded up on rocks. Crouching, they headed through tall yellow grass toward the higher bushes. They were trying to be quiet and not be seen.

—What are they..?

Sharon shushed me.

—We have to be quieter than them even. Come on!

We crawled through the dry grass. It crackled under our shoes. It was strange and thrilling to follow those three big boys.

She stopped me with a hand on my shoulder. She pointed for me to look.

I rose up to see the three older boys crawl along the ground like snakes. They stopped.

Rodney lifted himself up a little in the tall grass, like a soldier in the movies.

—There she is!

—Is it her? said the skinny boy.

—Yeah! Get as close as you can, then let her have it!

I raised up in the high sticky grass to try to see who was their target. I couldn't see anything. Were they pretending?

Sharon hit me hard with her elbow. She pointed in another direction.

—There!

All I saw was a little cat, grey with dark stripes. She had white feet and a small white mask around her eyes. She was pawing at a butterfly in the long grass by the bushes. She'd turn on her side and swat at it and the butterfly would flutter away from her claws then back close again. She seemed to get angry and swatted hard. She dropped to her side and licked her paws as if she'd caught the butterfly that was still floating around her head.

—Kitty! said Rodney.

—Here pretty pussy!

—Here Sharon! Here girl!

I turned to Sharon, but she elbowed me hard in the side. Her face was set in a strange way as she watched those three.

The cat lifted its head at the boys' calling but went back to its game with the black and orange butterfly.

—Okay, fan out.

—Now!

Rodney and his friends stood up. They spread out about fifteen feet apart. Crouching, they ran at the cat. They raised their arms.

They closed in on the cat.

—We got you now, Sharon! We got you now!

—Dead to rights, you little bitch!

—We got your ass!

The cat was slow to react. She looked up and watched the boys running at her as if this were part of her game.

—Run, kitty! I said under my breath.

Oh god, I wanted to yell it! I wanted to yell it out so loud the kitten would move on the sound waves of my shouting as characters sometimes did in cartoons.

She tensed her body. Her ears went up.

Rodney threw the first rock.

—Sharon! Now you'll do what—

—Little bitch! Whore!

The boys came together around the cat. Throwing rocks as fast as they could. She was cornered.

—Now you're going to get it!

■

All three reloaded with rocks from their pockets. All three threw at once.

The rocks were headed right for her. The kitten did the stupidest thing. She ran right at them.

Rodney reached down for her as she ran by his big ugly boots. But she veered away and out of his grasp.

He jumped to stomp her. He seemed to catch a piece of her tail, but now the little cat was really running, sprinting, past the boys and having a wonderful time running away from everything in the world.

Rodney took the rest of the rocks out of his pocket. One by one he fired them right down into the ground at his feet as hard as he could. And with each one he swore and said a worse word than the last. Then he started putting the words together in combinations.

His friends did the same.

—What'll we do now? Go home? See if the bitch is there?

The blonde boy with the big red marks on his face looked back the way we'd come as he said this.

Sharon and I ducked down into the dirt and rocks. It seemed to me the boys were tall enough to look down into the grass and see us.

It was very quiet, silent except for the sounds of a mockingbird making all the noises it heard in the neighborhood.

—It's okay, came Rodney's voice. I got her picture right here in my pocket. Let's go over there into the trees and do it.

We didn't hear their steps, but we did hear the sounds of them prying their way through the bushes where they'd tried to trap the kitten. Palm trees circled a clearing, as if a house had once been there and then was taken away. Two pines grew nearby and the three big kids went into brush around those.

—Should we? I said.

Sharon shrugged.

We crept up behind one of the palms. We could hear them saying her name and swearing. There were other sounds too.

—Let's write down how many times they say each bad word.

She nodded and took out the crime book and I took out my notepad. We each scribbled just as fast as we could to keep up with what they were saying.

—Cause she's such a stupid bitch.

—Nothing but a dumb, ugly...

They kept saying Sharon's name, adding things I didn't understand. A few I did. What they said and the way they said it was terrible. It made my stomach upset and made me angry in a way I'd never felt before. I was mad for myself, but I was madder for Sharon. I felt their words killing her. I wanted to make those big boys feel worse than they were making her feel.

Sharon didn't seem to be watching. I tapped her shoulder

—I think I see how your brother's like Mr. Gaylord, I said. Why did they call the cat your name? What are they doing to your picture?

She shook her head.

—They're not important, she said. They're not important at all. We're important, you and me. We're all that counts in the whole wide world.

—Really?

—Really.

I wanted to stand up and turn around and show myself to the sun and to the wonderful sky.

Sharon clamped a hand on my shoulder to keep me down.

Then she turned her body around to face me. She took both my ears and held me low and close to her.

—You remember what you said that you wanted to do to me the other day?

I pulled my face away from her. I had told her about what

I wanted to do to her when I saw her make her handstand in my driveway that Tuesday afternoon. But as soon as the words got out of my mouth I had wanted to stuff them right back in. Now, she had found the right time to tell me off. She was going to say I was like these others, her brother and the other two roughneck boys. She was going to tell me how horrible I was. That if I wasn't such a chicken I'd be just like them.

—Are you going to listen to me or not? she said.

—I guess.

—Well, she said, one day you were calling Mr. Cary's dog to give him a little piece of meat you had leftover from your dinner. I was behind the fence watching you. *Good dog,* you said when he took the meat from your hand. *Good dog.* And you fed him with one hand and petted him with your other hand. Well, I had this sudden feeling about you. All of a sudden, I wanted to smash your head and tear your clothes down from your shoulders and down around your waist so you couldn't move your arms and down lower so that you were paralyzed. Then I could do anything to you, anything I wanted to do. Anything at all.

—Really?

—Really. And that's a million times worse than what you wanted to do to me. In fact, I'm not sure what I wanted to do to you exactly, except it was really terrible, more terrible than anything *you* could ever imagine. And, for me, it would be the best thing that would feel better than the best thing there was in the world.

—Really?

—Really.

While we were talking, Rodney and his friends had left. We were alone out there in that field with all that high dry grass and trees.

—

TWELVE

A new family moved in down at the end of the block. They had two children, a boy and a girl, both about Sharon's age. I saw Mr. Tammerand walk Sharon down the street toward the new kids' house. He was wearing his black suit and had his big hand on her shoulder. I watched out the side window.

After that, I didn't see her for two days.

My father was eating a bacon, lettuce, and tomato sandwich and trying to hold it so that it didn't drip on the shirt he'd had to iron the night before. My mother's new kind of headaches were worse again and light hurt her eyes. Late at night when I guess maybe the pain wasn't quite as bad, she got up and did things for us for the next day. She usually remembered everything to do, even the smallest details, like napkins and ironing and socks; but sometimes there was something dad or I wanted that she didn't guess at.

—Where's that cute little girl that comes around here all the time? dad said. You know, the tomboy with the pretty hair? The one who pushes you around like you're married?

—

I opened my mouth but after a few seconds I closed it because I didn't have anything to say.

That afternoon I decided to go down to the end of the block.

The sidewalk seemed pretty dangerous. Too easy to be seen. So I sneaked around houses. An old man on a porch yelled at me to get out of his bushes. He thought I was a burglar. So I stayed behind walnut trees that grew near the sidewalk. I went from one tree to another.

I heard kids' voices when I got to the corner house. The fence went all the way around. I found a place behind a hedge and against the trunk of a big old dead walnut tree where I could listen without being seen by anyone.

It sounded like they were fighting. It sounded like something Sharon and I would do together. Sometimes we played a rough game of tag or a hitting game. She was doing it with these other kids.

I peeked through a knothole in the fence. There was a swing set and a rubber swimming pool with swans and ducks painted on it. There were children's shovels and pails, the kind you take to the beach and make sand castles with. I couldn't see anything else.

—Ouch—don't! said a boy's voice. Please don't!

—Why not?

It was Sharon.

—It hurts! It hurts!

—Do you want to play with me or not?

—Yes! Yes! said a girl.

—If you want to play with me, you have to show me what you can do.

—But I don't like this, said the boy.

—I told you what you had to do, Sharon said. You said you could. Now show me.

—I can do it, the girl said. I can.

—

—All right. Then get into the pool with your brother and tie this rope on your wrist and foot real tight. Tight as you can get it.

I shifted down to another knothole where I could see more of the little rubber pool. There was a funny-shaped boy maybe a little older than me kneeling in the pool. His arms were tied behind him with a jump rope. His legs were in the pool, but I could see that his ankles were also tied together somehow.

Sharon leaned against a pogo stick and watched the girl tie her wrist to her ankle.

Sharon lifted the pogo stick. I thought she was going to do some great trick. She swung the stick around past her chest and stuck the rubber tip end that you're supposed to use to bounce on right into the boy's chest.

—Ouch. No, please, don't *do that* any more. Isn't there some other thing I can do so I get to play with you?

—No. You have to do this first. Ready?

—Oh, please!

I could see from Sharon's shoulder to her knees. She kept the pogo stick raised. Then she turned to the girl.

—Okay, give me the rope.

Sharon took the rope that connected the girl's wrist and ankle and put the pogo stick through it. Then she lifted. The girl came up out of the pool, half balancing on her untied foot, half swaying on Sharon's stick. She was a very pretty little girl, blonde with short hair and nice little shoulders. She was wearing a yellow polka-dotted swim suit. Wet, the girl tottered in the sun where Sharon held her by holding the pogo stick against her side. The little blonde was like a fish out of water, flopping, fighting to live.

Sharon let her fall back into the shallow water. A big splash.

The girl sputtered, angry.

—You tried to drown me! You—

—

—Are you afraid of drowning?

—My mother told me never to take foolish chances around water.

—Who do you want to play with—your mother or me?

The girl pouted with her mouth and chin. She folded her arms and raised her head like she was going to give a speech.

—Oh, all right! she said. You're sure you've got a secret cave with a cabin and everything?

—You saying you think I lie, Nancy?

—No. But if you ask me, I think you're pretty bossy!

—Okay, Sharon said. You have to trust me. I want you to go under.

—Put my head under? But my hair'll get wet and mom—

—That's not important. I'm going to help you stay down with this underwater gun. Don't try to come up before I let you. On the count of three. One, two—now!

The blonde girl pinched her tiny nose with her free hand and dropped to the shallow bottom on her stomach. Sharon rested the pogo stick lightly on her little behind.

—And you—you're next. Or are you a cowardly dumb fraidy-cat?

The brother closed his eyes and let out a little moan. Then he headed for the dark blue bottom not far from his sister.

Sharon balanced at the edge of the wading pool, then stepped inside it. It was only a few feet deep, but she had the boy and girl down on their bellies so that their heads were under the surface. Sharon held the girl down with the pogo stick and kept one foot on the boy's back.

Pretty soon the boy wanted up, but Sharon kept her foot on him. He struggled and wriggled so that he could get his head just above the water by pushing his tied hands against the rubber bottom and raising himself on his arms as far as he could, arching his head and neck.

■

Sharon lifted her foot to his neck and he was under again.

Now the girl made a gesture with her free hand that she wanted up.

—Not yet, Sharon said.

I didn't think the girl could hear her.

I had taken a higher knothole. I saw the girl panic under the water. She twisted and shook and fought like some animal that knows it is about to die. Sharon was very good at keeping her down with the pogo stick.

I heard something, something strange and out of place.

It took me a while to realize why Sharon had her mouth scrunched down in her chest. She was making her laughter quieter that way. Something was funny to her.

This wasn't the Sharon I knew. Not in any way. We had played rough, but nothing like this. Maybe I was glad she had these two to play with from now on if this was her new idea of fun.

The boy struggled up, frantic, fighting now. Sharon pulled back her foot and kicked him in the jaw. It wasn't a hard kick, but he came up screaming.

—Let me out of here! You're trying to kill me! You're trying to kill me!

He climbed up and, tied as he was, tried to pull himself out of the pool.

Sharon shoved against his backside so that he slipped and lost balance and was face down in the water again.

The little girl had battled up and out while Sharon concentrated on her big brother. The girl sat beside the pool. She looked almost happy. She watched her brother thrashing around. Sharon wasn't even touching him anymore. The heavy boy was so upset that he kept tripping himself up when he should have been careful about the ropes and lifted himself out slowly.

Nancy raised her wrist and ankle gracefully, like the start of a trick.

—I won, she said. Now I get to play with you. Roger'll have to go find someone else...

—No. Now you and him trade places. Now you get to try what he did.

The girl dropped her tied hand and put both hands on her hips.

—Now, wait a minute. You promised that if I passed all the tests, you'd play with me. I passed the tests.

—You passed one test. Kind of. You've got about...let's see, about a hundred and seventy-two left. Want to get started?

The girl looked dumbfounded. Her brother, half-drowned, dragged himself out of the wading pool, spilling most of the water into the little flower bed under the rear window of the house.

—How could there be so many tests?

—There just are.

—I don't... I don't know.

—If you don't know, it's over.

—No one could pass all those tests.

—You're stupid, Sharon said.

—What do mean I'm stupid?

—Because a boy I know passed every one of them. He lives down the street.

Nancy kept her hands on her hips.

—You say I'm stupid, she said. I say *you're* stupid. And I think you should go play with the stupid kid down the street— if there really is such a kid. I don't see why *anybody'd* ever want to play with you.

—Maybe I will, Sharon said.

—Maybe you should go right now.

—Maybe I will, Sharon said.

—I don't even think there is a stupid boy down the street who passed all your stupid tests. I think you made him up.

—I did not make him up. He's my friend.

—If there was a boy who lived down the street who was a friend to a big stupid cow like you, why are coming around here bothering us?

I'd never seen Sharon throw a punch. When she and I wrestled and fought, it was elbows and body against body. Lots of tumbling and using your weight on the other person. But Sharon seemed to know that she was in a different part of the world here. Different tactics were called for. She walked right at the girl as she pulled her hand back into a fist and then she put it right into the girl's face as if she meant to go right through her.

There was a soft wet smack. Wet but hard. Then dead silence.

The brother was untying himself.

The girl picked herself up, rubbing her cheek.

—You're in big trouble. I'm telling *my dad*.

—I'm telling my dad.

—My dad is a cop, Nancy said. He's going to arrest you. Do you know what happens to girls when they put them in jail? Do you know, huh? Huh?

Sharon laughed.

—You're funny. I never would have played with you two idiots anyway. You're stupid and boring.

—*You're* stupid and boring!

Sharon headed for the fence, almost straight up to me. I hadn't noticed the gate that I'd worked myself toward as I went from one knothole to the next. I was right next to it.

I heard Sharon stop and use some of her brother's words on Nancy and Roger.

I ran. I ran all the way home down the middle of the sidewalk.

■

It was mid-morning, but dad was already down the street at Mr. Gaylord's house. He carried his typewriter down there almost every day now. Two mornings ago mom woke me up early to say that she had to go to San Francisco to look after her mother. It was getting to be too much for Aunt Regina. Mom's eyes were wet when she asked me to be good and promised to see me soon. It was weird, but that very same day it was almost like dad moved out and moved in with Mr. Gaylord.

Sharon and I had the house to ourselves, but it seemed too big for us somehow and made us feel uncomfortable.

—He's here, Sharon said. He's got to be here.

We were down in our basement. We really weren't supposed to play down there because of the dirt floor and walls. We had closed the two heavy halves of the slanted wooden door that fit together. We pulled on the little light, a hanging bulb at the end of a string. The basement had concrete steps going down and concrete floor and dirt everywhere else. We could easily stand up right under the back porch. But as you went to the front of the house, you had to crawl if you wanted to go all the way to the tiny window that peeked out onto our front garden.

The dirt on the sides was hard-packed and built up like shelves.

—Look, Sharon said. The finger man is back!

I laughed. I felt happy whenever she brought back an old game or character.

—Don't laugh, she said. This is serious today. Very serious. Finger man says sit down.

Sharon pushed against my chest. I sat.

She put her hands on her hips and surveyed the basement.

—Finger man's looking for a little man, she said. He says this is a very, very, very important little man. He has to find him. It's a matter of life and death.

Finger man ran up Sharon's blue and yellow dress. He seemed to peer around from her shoulder, sighting. Then he ran down again. He jumped up and down on the dirt floor. That meant he was ready to talk his funny talk.

—Me know where to find little man!

Finger man made a beeline for me.

—No!

I curled up with my knees together and my arms shielding my stomach.

—Must find! Must find!

Finger man was all over me. He'd never moved so fast before. His legs were light as spider legs, but strong and stiff as he trod my neck and shoulders and then my legs. He jumped on my rear end—until I rolled over on it—and he tickled my ribs and scampered back up to my face and chest.

—Lie flat! Finger man commands it!

—Tickles. Please, it tickles!

I was laughing. And I seriously wondered how angry finger man would be if I didn't go along with him.

—Lie down now. Flat! Flat for finger man!

Reluctant, I lay down on my back. I still had my knees pulled together and my arms crossed, ready to go anywhere on the front of my body where I might be tickled next.

Finger man walked along my arms. He walked down my stomach and I slid my arms lower so that they were crossed at the wrist.

—No, I, finger man command you, on forfeit of your life. Arms at your sides. Don't move, or you will die.

I did as I was told, but already I was giggling and squirming, even while finger man waited to continue his search.

—Still! Silent!

Finger man found that my red and white Tom Mix shirt had pulled up a little. He used one of his legs to pull it up farther.

■

—No moving!

Finger man grabbed the waist of my jeans. They were loose from lying on them. He pulled.

—Hey, wait!

Sharon loomed over me.

—Davy, this is serious. We have to let the finger man do what he needs to do or he's going to go away forever. He'll die, Davy. Forever. Is that what you want?

No. It wasn't what I wanted.

I lay still. It was an amazing thing. I hardly ever paid attention to my body, but finger man seemed fascinated by it. It took all my concentration not to squirm and giggle and protect myself by rolling over or pulling away.

Finger man pulled down my pants and my underpants.

—Hello, little man, he said. I knew I'd find you. I knew you were here somewhere.

—Hello, finger man, Sharon said in another voice. I've been waiting for you to find me.

—I've found you, little man, finger man said. Now we're going to be great friends forever and forever.

—That's right, finger man. And I'll always be here waiting for you whenever you need me.

—That's good, finger man said. That's very good. I think I can live a while longer now. I think I can live for just a little while longer now that I know where you are and how to get you to talk to me.

—That makes me happy, too, finger man.

The cold concrete under my back was warm now. It felt like fire.

When I sat up, finger man was gone. Sharon hummed something while scratching names and patterns in the dirt.

-

THIRTEEN

It was fun to see things that weren't there. To make them be there. I sent away with box tops for a Space Patrol Projection Light. Sharon and I would crawl into my closet and slide the door closed behind us. One little strip of film clicked into the carriage. You turned it on like a flashlight. The round picture came out on the white wall of the closet. It showed spacemen and women exploring other planets. We stared at each picture for a long time.

Leaving the closet for the ordinary world was always a big disappointment.

Sharon and I collected a series of cards that the kids at school thought were stupid because they wouldn't take the time to make them work. The idea of magic image cards was that you stared at this circle with a black and white scene in it reversed. What was supposed to be white was black and what was supposed to be black was white in the circle on the card.

The longer you stared without blinking, the better the picture would come out. You didn't need a projector or darkness.

A regular room with the shades open but with the lights turned off was best and afternoon was the best time to do it. We would squat on the floor and trade cards, each trying to beat the other in being the one to stare the longest without moving our heads. You had to keep very still to make the image clear.

Even after the time on the card's instructions was up—a minute or two—we went on, usually doubling, tripling, or quadrupling it. Then we'd stare at a blank wall. The picture the card had printed on our eyes came out on the blank wall. It was great because you didn't need anything but your own eyes.

—Endurance, Sharon said.

Her favorite new word.

—The one with the most endurance gets the best picture. The perfect picture. My picture is the most perfect of all.

—Tell me. Say what's in your picture. Describe the scene.

I watched Sharon sit back on her haunches, preparing herself. My picture, already fading, was all over her. Rocks around her waist and chest, saturn hanging in the sky around her ears, battalions of warriors over her entire body.

—It's a girl's face, Sharon said. She's very pretty. She has long hoop earrings. Her hair is up in beautiful curls all around her head. She has perfect skin and a perfect nose and mouth. She has the most beautiful eyes in the world. She's looking at somebody. She isn't sure who she's looking at. But looking at him makes her so happy and feel so funny that sometimes she thinks she's someone else.

Wow.

—What do you see? she said.

I didn't want to describe my scene after hearing her description. It didn't seem good enough, with its space rocks and dead planets. But Sharon seemed satisfied when I finally told about it.

That was the last time we ever played with those cards that you stared at and then looked at a blank place on the wall.

My dad was down at the other end of the street with his typewriter at Mr. Gaylord's.

We squatted on the den rug and stared at the door of dad's work room. We knew exactly what we had to do. We had been planning for months, ever since we read in her book about the importance of locked doors. We had even gone to the library and checked out books on how to do it.

> The exact number of tumblers must first be determined. Each tumbler must be engaged. If any one tumbler is neglected, the desired result will not be achieved. Simultaneity is generally of the essence here.

We each had our own ideas. We'd fiddled around with bathroom locks. Mr. Tammerand wondered how Sharon could lock herself out of the bathroom.

Sharon squirmed into place to eyeball the hole in the lock of dad's workroom.

—Me first.

She had a little needle she had taken from some things her mother had left behind. These things were special to her. She told me that she was sure the needle would do the trick.

—See? she said. It goes right in. Now... You wiggle it around and see...

I was nervous about my father coming back. I went to the front door, opened it, checked down the sidewalk both ways to see if anyone was coming, then hurried back to Sharon.

She hadn't moved. She had one eye squinted. The needle was in the lock. She worked it around in there so patiently. Over and again.

Even though I was sure my ideas were better, I hoped that she could do it. She had put so much into it. She loved that little needle. She had so much confidence that it would work. How was she going to feel if it didn't?

It was a long time before she stopped.

—I'm not giving up, she said. I'm just giving mom's needle a little rest.

She pulled it out of the lock.

The long silver needle was bent in several places. The tip had broken off.

—Oh, I guess it needs to be straightened out a little.

—I'll try now, I said.

I had a little plastic knife that came in a Cracker Jack box. I slid it in carefully. No. Too big. Next I tried a small screwdriver. I'd found it in the cellar in an old toolbox my dad got when his dad died. The head of the little screwdriver fit in exactly, with no room to spare.

—Sharon, look!

She looked, but she didn't say anything. She was still trying to fix her mom's needle. She seemed upset that it wasn't getting straighter.

I turned the screwdriver. Something was caught inside holding it back. I twisted it and worked it around.

—Whoops.

The tiny metal lips around the lock bent out of shape and kind of tore.

I had a hammer with me and tried a few light taps to get things back to normal. One side, then the other. Worse. Lots worse.

—We've got to find something that's small enough to go in there but hard enough to...

The front door!

It was my dad. He was home!

Sharon grabbed her things and scrambled to her feet. I crammed the tools in the back pockets of my jeans, mashing one finger and scraping my knuckles.

—Hi, kids. Hi, Sharon. Keeping cool in this heat?

We nodded. I was sweating. It trickled down the inside of my arm.

—Say—would you kids do me a favor? Could you got to the store for me and get a few things?

Mom never asked for favors, but dad always seemed to have chores for us that he couldn't fit into his day. We both nodded eagerly. I think we were also both happy to get out of the house, away from the locked door.

That night dad and I took a taxi to the bus depot and picked mom up. She kissed me and dad and kept asking over and over how we were doing. Then she was quiet almost the whole way home before she told us she'd have to go back in two days. Aunt Regina was *spelling her*, she said. But just for the weekend, and she'd have to head right back until...

Later, she came into my bedroom.

I felt an amazing, unexpected flood of relief that mom was going to tuck me in.

—Honey, can I talk to you a minute?

—Sure, mom.

—Davy, I want to tell you...

I knew she'd found the metal twisted on dad's locked door.

—I want to tell you how much I appreciate the way you've been acting.

I had no idea what she meant.

—What way?

—Oh, you know. I know it's hard for a young boy like you to be on his own so much. But you've been perfect, just perfect. And so has Sharon. Your dad and I are so proud of you. I think you two are so good for each other.

I couldn't look her in the eye. I couldn't look at her.

My mom gave a little laugh. She cleared her throat.

—Oh, I know her father wanted her to play with those neurotic little Hamilton children, but that's all over with now. Davy, you should have heard the crazy things those two katzenjammers said about Sharon. It would make you laugh.

—Yes, mom.

—Honey! You act like I'm bawling you out. I love you. I love you so much—

—Mom...

I almost said *you're crushing me*, except I liked it so much I was afraid she might stop.

—Oh, I'm sorry honey for being such an old silly. I just wanted to let you know how much I appreciate how mature and responsible you've been without me or your dad giving you any real supervision. You two just supervise yourselves, don't you? Well, you've just been wonderful.

—Thanks, mom.

—Well, you don't have to look so dismal about it! Smile when someone tells you you're doing a great job!

—He's got guns and weapons in there, Sharon said. Why else would he keep it locked all the time?

We were up in one of the biggest walnut trees on the block behind where we lived. There were three empty lots and a little drying shed. This walnut tree was easy to climb and had good wide limbs to sit on once you were up in it. It seemed like we were on top of the whole wide world.

—Maybe there's valuable stuff in there, I said. Gold and diamonds that he's keeping for the commonists.

—Your folks are poor, Sharon said. Besides, if he had small stuff like that, he'd keep it in a safe like my dad does. Then he wouldn't have to worry about thieves or *prying eyes*, like my dad says.

—Whatever it is, I said, it must be stuff Mr. Gaylord gave him.

Sharon pulled the green coat off a walnut and examined what she found. She seemed to agree with me.

—Things that have to do with movies, she said. My dad says Mr. Gaylord was so bad he got kicked out of Hollywood. My dad says he's on this list like they had in *Treasure Island*, a *black list*. Maybe your dad's on that list now. Hey, you think your dad's got a body in there?

I threw a dried-up walnut. It landed near the old water tower behind the Hamilton's yard.

—It'd smell, I said. No, what's in there is mysterious. That's why we have to find out what it is. If it's something bad, then we know. Otherwise...

—You still want to save your dad, don't you?

I nodded *yes*.

—Well, you can't. It's impossible. Nobody can save him. Can we try the lock again tomorrow?

I was glad she wasn't too discouraged about her mother's needle getting bent.

—Sure, I said. Tomorrow.

FOURTEEN

All morning I watched mom pack. It seemed important that I see everything she put into her suitcase and the little bag with a zipper and handle she called *toiletries*. I couldn't take my eyes off her. In the bathroom or her closet her eyes would go somewhere, settle on some thing. She would think a bit, and then either reach out and take it or go on to something else. A comb, earrings, a pair of socks. I followed, I watched. I was each of them, those items. I pretended it was me being packed and taken along.

Why was mom taking *so much*?

It took a long time for the taxi to come. For a while mom, dad, and I waited on the front porch. Then we went back inside. Around midnight the night before when they thought I was asleep, I'd heard mom and dad talking about whether or not we could afford another taxi round trip. For some reason, that made me kind of nervous now waiting for it to come. We watched the street. Mom and dad weren't exactly standing together. They were a little bit apart. I was too. We looked at each other. We all seemed to have questions that we couldn't ask or things we couldn't say.

The doorbell rang. The man standing on our front porch had an ugly beard with long hairs that were different colors. He pulled mom's bags from her hands so fast and hard that she stumbled. Dad and I followed her down the steps and watched her climb into the taxi.

—Goodbye, darling. I'll be back just as...just as soon as I can.

I knew I couldn't tell her to have a good time. I couldn't say I hoped grandma was okay. Mom was going away because she wasn't.

—Okay, mom.

My dad bent to the taxi window and leaned in.

The driver took his foot off the brake and my dad's head almost got caught inside.

—Hold it, buster! dad said.

Then I heard the little tinkling tune. She'll be coming round the mountain when she comes. She'll be coming round the mountain. And then *Turkey in the Straw*.

The Good Humor man! My new favorite was the Volcano Cone, with vanilla all down inside the long cone and this thick spill of chocolate and strawberry frozen over the top like lava.

And then the truck turned the corner onto our street. It was a tall white truck with stickers all over it saying the kinds of ice cream the man carried. He was dressed in white and he looked right at me as he rang the bell. The music was so loud I could hardly hear my mother.

—I know you two will do just great...

The taxi pulled away. I wanted an ice cream so bad. I waved mom away in her taxi, but I was watching the Good Humor wagon. I felt horrible as I watched the yellow car turn the corner toward the highway that would take mom to the bus depot. If only she knew. What would she think of her selfish little brat then?

I heard the ice cream truck turn to go down the next block. I thought of running after it, my hands making fists at my sides, stupid little weak fists.

I had them all lined up. My bedroom door was locked.

I hadn't wanted to put them on the bed. So I lined them up on the middle shelf of the stand that I kept my comic books on, all facing me. I stared at them for a long time, at each one alone and then all together.

Mom had not tried to put them out for the Goodwill since we'd moved to Axminster.

My men. What did I feel for them now? I thought of the part they had played in my life. I thought of life without them. Was that what I wanted now, life without them?

—So, Bozo, is this it? Mr. Bear? Little Bear? Stripey? I don't expect you to talk. You never talked, really. Just fought and had adventures. I talked in voices for you. You never knew what I was making you say. Now...

Now that I had them lined up as if they were on display, I was afraid to touch them. I wasn't a child anymore, was I? Wasn't I too old to play with dolls? I sensed that if I touched them something of my old way with them might come back. Or not. Maybe I was more afraid that I would touch them and feel nothing. Almost like watching my mom leave in the taxi with the Good Humor man coming. Nothing.

So I walked around them like some sort of inspector.

—So, what do you think? It's over, right? Everything is over?

Their eyes were buttons, glassy, fixed buttons sewed onto fabric with thick thread. But I knew that. I had always known that. Mom had sewn those eyes back on more times than I could count. But it had never mattered before, the fact that their

—

eyes were buttons. Now it mattered in a way I couldn't understand and didn't want to think about very much. And I knew how worn and very ugly they were and I'd never thought about that much either. But now I did. Now it was all I could think about.

Something had changed. Something in the world had changed. I wasn't sure I liked it.

These stupid dolls that had always...

I threw them back in their box. I walked through the house carrying the box. I took it to the front porch beside the cement steps. I left the box there. I shut the screen door quietly and went back to my empty room.

Maybe mom was right. Maybe I was different now.

It was our fourth time with dad's lock. Each of the other times took an hour or more and ended in failure. Now we'd been at it for five minutes or so. We took turns with a nail file I'd found in mom's drawer and a skinny piece of metal we'd found in grandpa's tool box. We'd tried every combination in our other attempts. We'd even heard clicks, like the lock was opening. We had a feel for what not to do.

It was all touch. Squatting on my ankles, I probed inside until the file was snug in there and wouldn't move too easily. Then I started to direct the skinny metal tool in a few of the ways that had worked before. Click. But never quite here. Click. And there. Pop.

I jumped up.

—Sharon, I did it! I did it!

We joined hands and danced around in a circle in front of the door. We'd worked on the lock so long that we'd stopped thinking about actually swinging the door open. Making that lock come free had become our goal.

But now we remembered.

We stopped dancing and looked around. We were going

into an adult room, a locked forbidden adult room. What if we were caught?

We fussed around with our tools and wiped our hands on our clothes. Then Sharon turned the knob and pushed. The door moved. We peeked in. Was someone in there just waiting for us to come in so that he could hurt us? The idea of such patience, of someone waiting so long for us to come to him, waiting and...

We pushed the door open the rest of the way.

It was just a room. A messy room with a desk like an office. We knew there had to be more.

—I'll look for shotguns, Sharon said.

—I'll look for explosives and swords. And remember what we read about printing presses? That's real important.

We were quiet and thorough. We picked up each book and seventy-eight rpm record and record sleeve, each elephant-tusk paper weight and magnifying glass and letter opener, picked it up, studied it all over, looked underneath, then replaced it exactly in its little realm of dust.

—What have you found so far?

—Lots.

—Really?

—Well, not much.

—Me neither.

Sharon went into dad's little closet. I admired how she was so precise and careful. I tried to imitate her in going through the drawers of his desk, sliding each out slowly so that the sound was ever so slight. I shuffled through everything. There was no gun in the desk, no knife, no sword, no time bomb or box of metal printer's type. All I found was a bottle in the bottom drawer that said Old Kentucky on it. It had about three inches of brownish yellow liquid left in the bottom. It was a big bottle. I didn't open the cap to smell it.

-

I stood up from the desk.

—Nothing, I said.

Sharon had climbed out of the closet. She stood in the middle of the little room with her hands on her hips. I thought she was very beautiful standing there, her face scrunched up in concentration. How unusual to be scared—dad might come and catch us—and still feel great. How wonderful Sharon looked and how professional she was there in that cramped room!

She raised one finger and scratched behind her ear.

—Spies and investigators all say that if you're looking for something and you don't find it, then it's right under your nose. It's staring you right in the face.

I pivoted to scan the room. Nothing was staring me in the face.

—It's here, she said. Did you look at any of this stuff?

On top of dad's desk were a bunch of papers. It was all very careless and sloppy.

—No! I said. That's it. It's all messy so the secret is right here in the mess!

—Exactly. Let's see what we can find.

We sat together on dad's desk chair. We were both big now, but still skinny enough to get our rear ends side by side on that seat.

—This says *The Pirates of Always*. What is it?

I took the stapled pages, ten or twelve of them. I had become more confident with reading just in the last six months or so.

—It looks like one of dad's radio plays. I don't think I ever heard this one, so maybe he hasn't finished it or hasn't sent it out to them.

—I thought you said he was writing movies?

I shrugged.

—What's this pink thing on top?

I pulled the half-page out from under the paperclip.

Dear Mr. DiGiorgio,

Thank you for thinking of American Broadcasting for your radio script *The Pirates of Always*. We find your narrative style and character delineation both pleasing and skillful. However, certain of the themes you touch upon are among those we find it necessary to avoid at this time, given the sensitive public reaction to any material that might be deemed less than patriotic or, to be blunt, un-American.

I want to tell you that I personally have always been impressed by the integrity of your work. I am quite sure that upon closer examination of your script, you will realize that our reservations are not without merit.

I sincerely hope that we will see a new script from you in the very near future. You are one of the bright lights of the American airways.

Sincerely yours,

Bertram S. McIntyre

—What is it? Sharon said. What's it mean?

I shrugged.

—I think it means we can copy it, you and me. We'll make our own copy. And then maybe you and I can perform an original radio story by my dad that nobody else has performed ever.

—Really?

Sharon gave a little excited jump.

—And what's this?

I took the neatly typed page from Sharon's hand. It had a man's name and an address at the top and dad's signature at the bottom.

Dear Dr. Shoeckler:

This is to inform you that the invoice you keep sending me for my wife's treatment in your office last month
is still in error. Please note the circled column where the
injection costing $4.75 has been mistakenly added again
to your final total. While I am eager to settle with you so
that we may continue to use your practice, I will not
remunerate until...

I read some of it aloud.

Sharon kept finding more stuff on dad's desk.

—What's this?

It seemed like a poem. The paper was old and brittle. My
eye dropped down to some amazing words. I pointed them out
to Sharon.

She squinted, shook her head.

—Long words make my eyes hurt. Read it to me.

I smoothed the paper and held it with both hands on my
lap.

> Your lips are honeyed drops at which I'll sup til dawn;
> Your legs are the wings I use to find the sky.
> Your breasts are sweet bowls from which I'll drink
> Til my bloods bursts into yours and I die in you forever.

—Wow. Sounds like your dad really loves your mom—or
somebody!

I set the poem down and covered it with the letter and
other papers. I didn't have any idea what the words meant, but
I felt that I had hurt my parents somehow by reading them.

—What's this?

Sharon shoved another sheet at me. It was handwritten.

> Abolition of all private property held primarily in land
> and the application of all financial gains acquired
> through renting of such land to be applied exclusively to
> public purposes.

This was neatly printed. There was a note out to the side of it.

> Maybe if these translations weren't so stuffy and stilted, more people would see the clear good sense in these ideas. Perhaps write my own translation of the translation? (I.e., #1 could read: Do away with private property and give rent money to the people. Not bad.)

—Look at this, I said. Sharon, I think this is something...
—Wait. What's that?
But we'd both heard it, a lurching sound of wood on wood. The front door!

Crazily, like scampering thieves, we tried to put everything back as it had been. Sharon closed the closet door. I scattered the papers on the desk. We ran to the door and locked it behind us.

Nothing.
The house was empty.
Except for us.

FIFTEEN

—It'll be our little secret—won't it, Davy—having Tom here tonight? I don't know why your mother doesn't like him.

And, of course, your friend. She's always here for my...*debuts*.

Dad laughed. He seemed happy about something tonight. That was unusual these days.

Mr. Gaylord came in with a big bottle of what I thought was water. It was clear and you could see right through it. He also had a little brown bag.

I followed him and dad into the kitchen. Mr. Gaylord took out a carving knife. He pointed the knife at my dad.

—Want you to try something new tonight, Gray. Look. You cut your lime in half, see? Now, you hold it in your left hand, okay? Now lick the back of it. No, no, the back of your left hand—that's it. Now—

Mr. Gaylord sprinkled salt onto the back of my dad's hand where he'd licked. He did the same to himself.

—You're set. Now you do like this. You take a bite of your lime, a lick of your salt and then—

Mr. Gaylord turned the bottle up into the air. His Adam's apple bobbed up and down like a ping-pong ball.

—Gahhh! Smooth! Now you.

Dad bit the green fruit and licked the salt stuck on his hand as Mr. Gaylord said. He looked at the mouth of the bottle. I knew he was waiting for Mr. Gaylord to look away so he could wipe it off with his sleeve or a washcloth. Dad wouldn't even drink out of my glass or my mom's glass or use our silverware if we were running out of clean.

But Mr. Gaylord kept watching and finally dad lifted the bottle and drank. His adam's apple was smaller and it seemed to get snagged midway in his throat. He gagged and spray came from his mouth.

Mr. Gaylord nodded as if this was exactly the way he had figured it was going to happen.

—Well, he said. That's a start. How's my script coming?

Dad was still coughing a little. He wiped his eyes and mouth.

—Davy, he said. Would... Would you go next door and get her now? It's about time.

I didn't like to go next door when Mr. Tammerand or Rodney were home. They got mad and yelled if they heard me tapping on Sharon's window. But if I knocked on the front door, they always answered before Sharon did and acted like I was bothering them in some awful way.

Sharon sat on the wooden steps of their front porch. She wore her purple and pink dress with the lace at the waist and the sleeves. She had her head propped in her hands like she'd been waiting for a long time.

—I love your smile, she said as I came up the steps.

Her hand came up to my face and it seemed easy enough

to let her touch my cheek. Then I thought about where we were and pulled back.

Her face fell, but her eyes stayed on me. I'd never seen her like this.

—It's tonight, she said.

—Yes, tonight's my dad's program. He thinks you're always there—like good luck or something. But I remember...

—That's not what I meant. Tonight, Davy.

I shrugged. She grabbed my hand. She swung my arm. We walked that way up the porch to my house. I thought once we dropped hands to close the door, that was it. But she grabbed my hand again and started swinging it and walked me that way to the kitchen where dad and Mr. Gaylord were eating their lime and licking salt and drinking from the same bottle.

They looked at us and said nothing. They passed the bottle and salted themselves up again.

—Got to be pre-pared when you got a big screening, Mr. Gaylord said.

—Screech-ing? Ear-ing? dad said. An old *air*-ing—that's all I ever get.

Sharon and I looked at each other, a long look. It felt strange to be holding hands right in front of my dad and this other man and them not even noticing or saying anything. It felt bad in one way. We were not important to them, not right now. But in another way it felt safe and good, as if we were invisible. As if we could do anything right under their noses.

Being summer, it was still light. But by the time the show came and dad closed the curtains in the den, it was dark enough.

—What the hell you doing, Gray? Drank so much you're goin' blind?

—Just a precaution, Tom. I mean a transition. A tradition. If you listen in the dark, you listen with more... You listen with...

—Focus, dad.

—That's it, Davy. Focus. You focus on...on the true message that the story conveys to *you*, the listening audience.

Mr. Gaylord made a funny sort of mean laugh down in his throat.

He and dad sat in the two easy chairs facing the radio.

Sharon and I sat on the floor, still holding hands.

The radio tubes began to glow. Dad always kept the sound turned down on the show that came before. He never wanted anyone to get so interested in whatever came on first that they didn't give their full attention to his program. The station break came and the announcer said the network name.

Dad started to get up to turn up the volume, but he didn't try hard enough and fell back into the chair. He laughed, then looked confused. I dropped Sharon's hand and got up to turn the radio up real loud. Anything to keep dad's good mood.

—Thanks, son. I'm a little...a little bit inc-ca-paci-tated. The libations provided by my friend...my friend...

—Tonight's episode on *Dimension X* is *A Glimper of Truth* by Graham DiGiorgio.

Sharon's hand was in mine again. That made me happy as I settled down.

It was important to listen. Sometimes dad asked me questions later. Did I understand the theme? Did I see what he was trying to put across? I never did, but he wanted proof that I'd listened.

—Son, you want to make me proud, don't you?

It startled me. But the voice from the radio wasn't dad's voice, just one that sounded a lot like it.

—Here, son, the Lorvnaac family weapon; Redeemer, we call her. She's almost the first vaporizer made here on Ganymede, but she's killed many a Glimper. In the hands of a fine strong boy like you, she'll kill many more.

-

—I can't accept this wicked weapon, father. I don't hate the Glimper. I don't believe in war. I don't believe in killing anything.

Sharon made the finger man dance up in my face.

—I should listen, I said.

—No! she said.

Sharon grabbed my hand. That was fine. I could hold hands and listen too.

—No, this!

She bent my fingers. She pulled my hand around until the fingers were pointing down. Then she made the two middle fingers stay long, with the others curled up.

—But you said there's only one finger man, I whispered.

She shook her head. She seemed more upset than angry.

—This is special, she said. From now on we share. Your finger man has to find something. Like my finger man found something in the cellar. *And* you have to tell me something.

—What?

—Do you want me to scream?

—No!

My dad and Mr. Gaylord seemed to be listening to the radio play.

—Find the most important thing. You have to tell me. You have to say it.

I made finger man walk the floor between us. He wanted us to hold hands. But Sharon's hand came up flat to stop him. She made him stand on the hardwood floor. She made him be still. Then her finger man jumped up. He went to her leg and climbed. He went to her knee. He gently raised her dress on her crossed leg. Her body was changing a little, I thought, but not like the big kids yet. But now that I saw her leg I thought it looked almost like a woman's leg. Like the leg of a lady swimmer I had seen in newsreels. Sharon grabbed my wrist and led my hand.

She took finger man under her dress. Would he discover cities, people, forests, and castles?

—On Ganymede, there is no greater disgrace than this. That you, Thratle, son of Gustar Lorvnaac, would refuse to take into his hands the sacred Redeemer. Son, there is no greater glory than to die for the good of your world, your people, your species. I cannot believe that you will force me to go before the Great Magnetic Council of Ganymede and say that I...

—Farther, Sharon said. *Underwear.*

I loved the touch of the skin of her legs. I was scared at how good it felt. The finger man stopped after every couple inches of headway. He hopped around a little as if he was doing something there that he thought was important. As if he'd forgotten that he was supposed to keep going. But Sharon reached in and yanked my wrist. I moved him up another inch or two, then back a bit. I was afraid of what the finger man would find if he traveled too far.

—Underwear, she said.

Finger man danced in place. He hoped it was good enough.

—Do you want me to scream? she whispered.

Finger man flattened out against her leg and moved along the smoothest surface ever felt.

—What does finger man think he is, a butterfly? Sharon said.

There was something wonderful about the space that separated her legs. Something wonderful about the feeling that finger man was going to find out something very important that he had never known before.

—And so, Lensentinel Gustar Lorvnaac, you tell me that the most direct descendant in your lineage refuses the sacred gift of the family weapon? You know the punishment, Gustar.

—Please, My Lord, not banishment to a penal asteroid to work alongside those foul Glimpers we are sworn to kill! Please, I will detain him myself in our own domicile. But not...

—

—You know that it must be.

—*Underpants*, she said.

She took me by the wrist and showed finger man the elastic.

He felt how tight the elastic was to her skin. It dug into her. It was like part of her skin, as if it was attached. Finger man was scared to pull on it for fear of pinching or ripping her skin.

But then something happened.

Sharon touched me.

The world went away.

It seemed to come up from the toes of my crossed feet and to travel up my spine and out of my head. I was up above my own body. It was the most amazing wonderful thing I'd felt. Just like when she did her handstand in the sunset—except maybe almost better. It was like she was doing the handstand with her body against mine. And she stretched me and made me feel as sleek and perfect as she was when she did it.

I touched her ear with my mouth.

—Would you do a handstand for me again so I could watch you do it?

She pushed me away.

—We're too old for that stuff. Where's finger man? I can't feel him.

My eyes were closed. I thought of our yard, how we parted the big leafs of the elephant plant and played inside. It was like a jungle or another planet, except even more real. It was like telling the truth about the electric meter with our life and death inside it.

Sharon really was more than my playmate and friend if we trusted each other with such great secrets. Finger man stayed where he was.

—What's he think he's doing? Sharon whispered.

—Exploring, I said.

—Does he like it?

—Yes. He likes it...very much.

—And you? Davy? Say...

I bit my tongue.

Finger man retreated to my face. I smelled something, like a trace of smoke from one of Mr. Tammerand's huge cigars that took all day and all night to smoke.

—Long years passed on the prison colony of Alixar VIII. Young Thratle Lorvnaac, citizen of Ganymede, labored amongst the Glimpers who were long-time prisoners of war. He worked with the goodness and dedication of a consecrated monk.

—You should conserve your energy, friend Thratle.

—For what, friend Grangt? I must do my share. It is the least I can do for the atrocities my people have inflicted on yours.

—But one man cannot...

—The sound of a rocket in distress resonated in the atmosphere. An almost human cry of metal heated and compressed to the very limit of endurance.

Sharon grabbed my hand and made finger man retrace his steps.

—What's that, friend Grangt?

—The ship of the Exalted Ruler of Ganymede. It's time for his routine inspection of all prison satellites.

—But the ship is in trouble. It's...oh, no, it's crashing. Quickly, we must...

—Thratle rushed to the site, and there, its nose half-embedded into the great Alixar plain, the ship of the Exalted Ruler of Ganymede.

—Burning, burning! The great ship is ready to explode! We must save as many of these unfortunates as we can!

—But, Thratle, think! These are the very ones who sentenced us here! Left you to die with we Glimpers, whom they despise above all.

—Still, they are human beings, no matter what their flaws and transgressions. They must be saved!

—I'll stop you! I won't let... Oh, no, he's running straight into the flames. He'll kill himself! Thratle, no!

—You have to say! Sharon said. You have to say without me telling you what to say.

I knew, of course. Maybe I'd known from the first moment I saw her out on the sidewalk walking past our house, her long brown hair bouncing high in sunlight.

—Oh, lord, Thratle sacrificed himself for his tormentors. I thought only we Glimpers were capable of such magnanimity. He was a true human being.

But I didn't think I could say it. It was too adult. She would make fun of me. Something terrible would happen if I said the words.

She turned her face into mine. It was red and angry. She reached down and grabbed my stomach hard, pinched and twisted.

—Do you hate me?

—No, I said. No!

—Then say it.

—I...

Sharon twisted the skin of my stomach so hard I could hardly breathe.

—I...I like you, I said.

She kissed my chin. Her hand eased its grip on my belly.

—There.

I sighed. We were saved.

We held hands.

—So the kid dies a martyr to what he believes? Mr. Gaylord said. And this alien sort of thing sees that—?

■

He looked around for the bottle of clear liquid.

—What is this, Gray, some kind of allegory or parable or shit like that?

—Exactly, dad said.

—And that's the same with this crappy draft you showed me that's supposed to be my movie?

—Ours. Sure, Tom, on the surface it's a circus film. But with a clown CO standing up against rampant militarism, represented by the circus owner and a black-listed acrobat refusing to turn in his friends and...

—Nope. No way, Gray. No symbols. No allegory crap. Everybody knows I've always been about saying what I mean and meaning what I say. Straight out. No beating round the bush.

—I gave up two years of my life, Tom. Is that straight out enough for you?

—You really were a CO?

—Yeah, my dad said. He sounded proud.

—Two years?

—Didn't see my son get born. Didn't see my wife. My baby was grown into a boy before I ever knew him.

—No shit?

—No shit.

Dad and Mr. Gaylord licked their hands and salted themselves again. They had lost or used up the lime. They licked the salt and drank some more.

They had almost finished the bottle.

SIXTEEN

—Hi, honey.

—Hi, mom.

—How are you, Davy?

—Fine.

I wanted to ask how grandmother was, but I wasn't sure what to say.

—You and dad are doing okay?

—Yes, mom. Hey, did you hear dad's story last night?

She didn't answer. The phone seemed to get heavier in my hand.

—Mom?

—What, honey?

—Did you hear dad's story on radio?

—Yes, honey. I heard it. It was sad.

What was sad about it?

—When are you going to be home, mom?

—I'm not sure. But school's starting in a couple weeks and

■

we have to get you some clothes. I suppose you and your dad can do some shopping?

—Sure, mom.

—Everything's okay? You're eating enough and getting your sleep?

—Great, mom. Everything.

—And how's Sharon?

How was Sharon? What could I say? I had to give my mother some sort of answer.

—She's fine, I said.

We had a place in her backyard. It was supposed to be a woodshed, but there was never any wood in it. We cleaned it up and made it our bungalow. It had chairs and a rug and books and pictures on the wall. An old sheet hung across the front made a good door.

I hadn't meant to surprise anybody.

But the voices from inside our bungalow stopped me outside the door sheet. No one ever went in except me and her.

—I've been wanting to talk to you for a long time, Sharon.

It was a man's voice. Her father? I didn't think he could fit under the low ceiling. Or Rodney?

—See, that stuff that your brother makes me do, I don't go along with that stuff. I mean, I'm there with him, but I don't want to be. Do you see what I'm telling you?

—Yes. I see what you're saying.

I sat down outside to wait. It seemed polite.

—Last school year I watched you sometimes. You probably never noticed. I watched you play baseball. We get in trouble if we come on your school grounds cause they don't want us ninth graders getting in fights with you little guys. You're really good, Sharon. You hit the ball better than any of the other girls.

—I'm big for my age.

—Not just that. You're very, ah, co-or-da-something. What's the word? Anyway, I always watched you playing. Followed you home sometimes, too.

—You and Rodney and the other one?

—No. Only when they weren't around.

Something in his voice—and the way Sharon's voice sounded when she answered him—made me get up from where they could see me if they stood up and came out through the sheet. I went around to the back, behind the rough wooden boards.

—Do you think we could do something? I mean like when you don't feel like messing around with that skinny little kid?

—What do you want to do?

—Oh, whatever. I mean, maybe we can think something up? What do you say, we get together and think something up to do?

—I'll think about it, Sharon said.

I didn't know how to feel about her answer and the way she said it. Only I was glad that I was hiding when the two of them came out of our bungalow.

It was the boy with the big red blotches on his face. He was wearing a low-necked undershirt that showed most of his strong chest and shoulders and he had the red spots there, too. The spots seemed angry and mean. He was a head taller than Sharon, and I thought I recognized his voice from a time when she hadn't been there to walk me home from school.

—I'll see you real soon, huh?

He tried to reach for her hand. He missed. But I wasn't sure if she'd made him miss or he just wasn't very good at grabbing hands.

—Good morning, little man.

—Good morning, finger man.

-

129

Finger man moved when Sharon spoke. But little man didn't move. She didn't touch him, even though she did his voice for him.

—How are you today, little man?

—Oh, I'm just fine, finger man.

My job was to sit there and stay still and let finger man walk around little man and talk to him.

We were down in the canyon. Not very far, just a little under the ledge, but we were definitely down in it. In the last week we had found a way to use one of the big dead oak trees to climb down about ten feet. Right below the place where we used to stand and scream and throw rocks. There was a little hole in the dirt wall that we made into a cave.

Nobody could see us.

—Little man, I have to say that I wonder about you sometimes.

—Why, finger man?

—It's how you look.

—How do I look?

—You remind me of one of those little mushroom men in that cartoon movie with all the music. Remember them? Except you don't run around. You just sit there. You never do anything.

That was my job. Just to sit like that. It had taken me a while to get used to it, but now it didn't seem any stranger than other games we'd played.

—Sometimes you look like a very short little man with a very big hat. Or a very bald man who just never grew up to have a neck or body or anything. How are we going to make you grow, little man?

Finger man jumped back and forth over the top of little man and said a few magic words we'd tried before. I always thought about the cow jumping over the candlestick, but little man was a candlestick burned down to almost nothing. The magic words never seemed to work the way Sharon wanted them to.

—Little man, little man, won't you get big? Won't you get bigger just for me?

I always tried to look cheerful and smile. But this stuff bewildered me. It was all out of my control and very frustrating.

I shifted my weight a little.

Sharon looked at me and shook her head.

—I'm bored. Let's do something awful and terrible and worse than horrible.

I pulled up my pants and stood up in the cave.

Sharon gave me her hand. I hung out over the edge. Before we found the cave, when we used to yell down into the canyon, the height scared me. I liked it now. I liked looking down there where my body would be smashed if I ever fell.

—Farther.

I inched out. My notebook was in my back pocket. I hardly needed it any more. The words had become part of me. Dad's radio play, every word of it—and other stuff we'd copied down from his locked room.

—Farther!

—Hold on tight!

—I got you, Sharon said.

—Free education for all children, I yelled.

—Louder.

I filled my lungs with all the air they'd hold. I loved this.

—All workers get an equal chance! I yelled.

—Scream, Sharon said.

—Workers of all countries everywhere unite!

I hung out into space. I had complete confidence in Sharon's strong grip. I pulled the notebook out of my back pocket. I scanned for what I wanted from the poems and other writing.

—

131

—Your breasts are clouds! I yelled. Your breasts are clouds floating in the pale pink sky!

—One more, Sharon said. Then it's my turn.

I shouted out several favorites. Then she squeezed my hand so hard that I had to end.

—Licking your toes! I cried. Licking your lovely long toes!

—I said it's my turn!

She pulled me back in. I dropped to my knees. As much as I liked hanging out there in space, it was a relief to be on solid ground again.

Sharon's turn thrilled me in another way. I was never certain that I could hold her for as long as she wanted to hang out there above the arroyo. We said it was hundreds of thousands of feet down, knowing it wasn't really. But it was far enough.

I held her at the wrist. I dug my heels in, all my weight back. There was a naked loop of oak tree root that was real strong. I held that with my other hand.

Sharon liked to be graceful and acrobatic about her hanging. The rules said you had to keep both feet inside the cave, which she did. She would start by letting her body simply fall outward so that I had to take all her weight with my hand. The first time I thought she was falling. And I was falling with her. Or would I have let go just in the nick of time?

The weight of her fall jerked against my hand. She waved her free hand. She didn't use her notes. She never seemed to need them.

—Radio and television and books and movies and newspapers, she shouted, all owned by the people's government!

Sharon waved her free arm like a girl in a golden swimsuit who swings from one circus perch to the next.

—Take everything from the aliens. Take liberties! Take liberties!

She was really swaying hard. How strong did she think I was?

—End the dreams of the rich! End the nightmares of the poor!

The thick oak root seemed to be loosening in the dirt that made up the walls of our cave. Pebbles and eye-watering showers of soil fell across my face.

—Hamgray is commonist! she screamed. And Mot Lordcow is commonist!

Hamgray and *Mot Lordcow* were code for my dad and Mr. Gaylord.

—Evad loves Norahs! Evad loves Norahs! We are not commonists! We are not!

—Sharon, it's time...

I tried to pull her in, but she stood on one foot now, swinging. Swinging out hard farther and farther over the canyon.

—Take liberties! Take them all!

I was scared. I was scared because I knew that sometimes she forgot that it was real. Everything that we were doing. Sometimes it seemed like she forgot what would happen if she fell.

—Little man and finger man are not commonists! she shouted. They are not cannibals! Cannibals! Cannibals! Cannibals!

Dirt showered down on my face. I held onto her big sweaty hand.

The first day we'd climbed down here and made our cave we'd screamed and thrown rocks at the man who lived in the arroyo. We'd heard him moving along the canyon floor beneath us. But it was not good enough. It wasn't fun enough and after that first time in the cave, we stopped.

Because now we knew all about the thing in the canyon. We knew all we wanted to know. We knew too much. But we

—

showed him we weren't afraid. We memorized dad's radio play that we'd found with the yellow note on it and yelled it down into the canyon. Sharon said it was never lost, that we had broadcast it out into the air forever and ever.

—Like ripples. Like ripples of water. That's what sound waves are. And they go on forever. Like our voices echoing in that dirty old bastard's ears down there. Forever and ever and ever and ever. So he can never forget what he really is.

SEVENTEEN

I heard their voices when I came in from the backyard. Then I saw them at the kitchen table. Two men and a woman. Was I in the wrong house?

—Course they'll save their asses, the woman said. They'll always save their own asses. That's what these people are, ass-savers. There's nothing else to them.

She was smoking. She slouched on our kitchen table as if she owned it and hated it. She had the driest, reddest skin I had ever seen on a lady's face. The two men were smoking too.

They had an old magazine on the table between them and they were taking turns smacking it with their hands and thumping it hard with their fists. *Time* it said in fancy print.

—Gary Cooper, Jimmy Cagney, Humphrey Bogart, said Mr. Gaylord. None of 'em knew I was even *alive* until HUAC. Then they start getting the third degree! And guess what? When the assholes can't even remember their own god damn name, Tom Gaylord's on their damn lips. See—see this? Jesus

Christ, they should give me some kind of award for't! *The guy most often named.*

The woman looked at him and blew smoke out of her mouth and nose onto him.

—They all turn on you, Tom.

—You can say that again.

—I don't understand it, my dad said.

He was smoking too, but instead of blowing out into the kitchen air like Mr. Gaylord and the woman, he blew the smoke down onto his hands holding the magazine.

—I just don't understand it. Norman Cousins, Whittaker Chambers—these are great men. Brilliant men.

The woman snorted a short laugh and blew smoke on my father.

—The smart ones turn pansy first, she said. They fall all over each other to grovel and whine and say everything they know—and then some.

I went to the sink and poured myself a glass of water. Dad nodded at me. He looked unhappy. I pulled my chair away from the table and sat down halfway in the dining room. I thumbed through a comic book, looking at the pictures.

My dad ran his wrist back and forth under his nose. His nose itched when he got nervous.

—Tom, are you sure? You really think more people will be going to jail? Actors, directors...writers?

Mr. Gaylord laughed a very ugly, cruel kind of laugh.

—Hell, GR-ay, if they send Dash Hammett to jail, why not you and me? You read *The Thin Man*? *The What-cha-ma-call-it Falcon*? He's the best, the goddamn best in this goddamn country. Maybe in the whole goddamn world.

My father looked into the rising smoke.

—I don't read thrillers, he said.

—Thrillers, Gray?

Mr. Gaylord looked quickly at the woman and they both laughed at my father.

—Gray, you read and write this sissy science shit? Mr. Gaylord said. And now you're going to talk *superior* to America's greatest writer?

The woman with the dry red face blew smoke over Mr. Gaylord's head and then down into my father's face.

—He's like the songbirds in this rag, Tom. He's superior all right, superior to his asshole. And that's what he sings out of.

—No, no, my dad said. I'm not saying that science fiction is better than the other forms of popular writing. It's just that I've found you can say more with it. Get away with more, in a manner of speaking...

—Say more?

Mr. Gaylord closed his eyes and blew a cloud of smoke up into the billows filling up our kitchen.

—Say more, DiGiorgio? Well, maybe that's going to be your name when they subpoena you—Say-More-DiGiorgio. Call the next witness, good old Say-More-DiGiorgio!

The woman snorted smoke and coughed out a thin little laugh that sounded like it hurt her throat. She had her eyes closed.

Mr. Gaylord rubbed his hand and arm slowly up and down her back.

—Me, I know how to handle these committee bastards, he said. You look 'em in the eye. They can't stand that, you know. You look 'em in the eye. You don't say nothing.

—Really, my dad said. I'm not one to talk about others. I've always been the kind of guy...

—Look 'em in the eye.

—That's right, honey.

—If they call me again, I'll go to jail before I'll give up one god damn name. Maybe the whole rest of mother-loving

—

Hollywood'll name Tom Gaylord, but when the newspapers come out, you'll see. Tom Gaylord don't name nobody. Nobody.

—Well, my dad said, when I was charged in my CO case and had to go before a hearing board to determine what they were going to do to me, they asked the names of all my *associates and friends*. I didn't give them one single...

The woman made a little noise down in her throat like she was crying. But then there was a look on her face as if she thought everything dad said was very funny. She stubbed out her cigarette, but her mouth stayed open in a peculiar way.

—My ex-here's a real man, she said. A real man.

Mr. Gaylord's chest swelled and he adjusted his cowboy hat to take another deep pull on his cigarette.

Dad snapped his fingers. Suddenly he looked happy.

—Hey, maybe you two should get back together!

—Together. Apart. It don't matter. She gets an itch or I get an itch, it don't matter. Always ends with the two of us shackin' up for a while—till we get to the point we can't stand each other no more and it's either murder or move on. Right, Virgie girl?

—Right, daddy.

The dry-faced woman looked dreamy now. As if Mr. Gaylord's words and his hand rubbing her back had put her to sleep. She kept moving her mouth a funny way, like she was always chewing something in one corner, something she didn't like. Or puffing on a cigarette that wasn't there.

—You're always so right, daddy. Ready to go homey-bye?

Mr. Gaylord put his head close to her heart and whispered loud.

—I might name you some names, Virgie—you know the ones you like to hear me say?

My dad picked his hand up off the table. I could see that it was wet on the back. He wiped it on his shirt. He started to put his hand back where it had been, but I think he saw where the moisture was coming from at the same time I did. He put his hand in his pocket. I didn't think the lady did it on purpose, but only because she kept puffing even when she didn't have a cigarette.

—Oh, daddy, she said to Mr. Gaylord, you have the dirtiest mouth I ever kissed.

They were almost out the back door when the lady came clomping back in on her thick sandles. She grabbed the magazine off our kitchen table and gave my dad an angry look as if she thought he meant to steal it from her.

She slammed the screen door and they were gone.

Dad turned and looked at me.

—Your mom called, he said. She says maybe she's coming home next week.

I wanted to ask if the yelling had anything to do with his and Mr. Gaylord's secrets.

—I've got a terrible headache, Davy. I'm going to lie down... You know better than to be a snitch, don't you, son? Selling out your friends is the worst thing you can do.

Dad got to the doorway of his room and then turned around and looked at me a long time.

—These are bad times, son. Bad times for smart people, for creative people. Bad times for anyone who ever thought about telling something like the truth.

He shook his head and disappeared into his room like a little boy.

I felt sorry for my dad. Things were hard for him. Things that I thought were pretty easy.

I went looking for Sharon.

■

Smoke again. Cigar smoke. It seemed to be everywhere.

I tried to hold my breath. But when I finally had to breathe, what I inhaled made me gasp and choke.

—When I first met you, David, I thought that you were a...well, an unreliable child. But in light of my daughter's recent assessments I've reconsidered that judgement.

Mr. Tammerand looked hugely satisfied with himself for being so flexible that he'd managed to change his opinion of me. He celebrated with another enormous intake of cigar smoke, which he finally exhaled over Sharon and me in equal portions as if it were some kind of special blessing.

—My daughter tells me of your plans for your future. These strike me as canny and well thought out. Remarkably prescient, I must say, for one so young.

Mr. Tammerand sat in the big brown padded chair. It looked smaller with him sitting in it. Sharon sat on the floor at his knee. I was on a piano stool facing him.

—Now, just what do you think you'll be studying in school? It's never too early to be thinking about which major you'll declare in college.

I was scared when Mr. Tammerand called me into the parlor. He almost never talked to me. The few times I'd waited inside for Sharon, he never looked at me or spoke or acted as if he knew I was there.

—Business management? Economic theory? Political science?

Mr. Tammerand took the cigar away from his chin and waved it in the air.

⟶ The inside of their house felt different from ours.

—Problem with political science departments these days is that your universities are run by reds. Instead of educating, they end up *indoctrinating*. In my day, there was a wonderful impartiality in any good undergraduate political science program. Very useful. *Impartiality*—do you know what that is, David?

I shook my head. I didn't know.

—It means that you are a big enough person not to just reflexively jump to one side of an issue. That first you consider all sides, not just the left-wing side.

He looked at me closely. He wore a blue vest and a grey tie. Except for a small brown mustache everything about Mr. Tammerand was big. His cigar was the biggest I'd ever seen. Mr. Tammerand looked very serious today, even more than usual.

I nodded.

He kept looking at me, so I smiled as I nodded.

—David, you don't want to turn out like your father, do you?

I wasn't sure how my father had turned out. I knew my dad hadn't finished living so that there still might be some more turning out for him. But it was a bad time for Mr. Tammerand to ask me this hard question.

I didn't like my dad having people in our house who insulted him and made him unhappy. I didn't like it at all. It made me mad at him.

—Well, David, you have a little stubborn streak, don't you? Sharon's been telling me about that, too. But you'd like to make more of yourself, wouldn't you? Don't you want to be somebody important, somebody who counts for something?

I didn't know what my face looked like, but I didn't want to be rude. I was afraid that he wouldn't let me be with Sharon any more if I made him mad.

—I don't know what I want to be, I said.

Mr. Tammerand cleared his throat. He turned his head and coughed into his hand. He knocked the ash off his big cigar.

I looked at Sharon. She was looking down at her folded fin-

■

gers, moving them a little. Why was it almost like she wasn't there at all?

Mr. Tammerand turned back to me. He lifted his hand in a fist, one finger pointed at me.

This room had newspapers in one corner and books in another. It wasn't like our house where there were little things like statues and flowers carefully placed here and there even though the rest was messy.

I wondered where Sharon's mom was. It was one thing she would never say.

—I find your attitude insulting, Mr. Tammerand said, wiggling his one finger at me. There's nothing wrong with being an investment banker. People like me run the lives of people like you and your father. And that's exactly how it should be. Right-thinking people like me should have power and control over those who are confused and bewildered about this brave new world we live in. Do you understand what I'm telling you, young man?

I smiled as big as I could and nodded fast and hard. I really wanted this to be over.

—You... Mr. Tammerand began.

He seemed to be thinking it over.

—Ah! he said. You're hopeless. You're as hopeless as Sharon. Lost, both of you. While others take the world by the tail—people like my son Rodney, a fine boy—you'll be spinning out of control with the other lost souls... Well, I've wasted enough precious breath on you.

Mr. Tammerand stood up. His knee brushed the side of Sharon's face.

I guess we were supposed to leave the second he did that. She started signaling, pointing toward the back door. But I found myself continuing to stare at him.

Sharon made a grab for my wrist but let go as if she was afraid to touch me.

Mr. Tammerand made a funny motion with his hand, his head turned away. He waved his hand down toward the floor several times. It was like he was telling a dog to get down off his leg. To disappear.

That's what we did. We disappeared fast.

EIGHTEEN

—You never make me scream.

We were inside the bungalow. I hadn't been in there in over a week, not since she'd been inside with what's-his-name who watched her play baseball and wanted to get to know her better.

—You scream all the time, I said. I hold you out over the canyon and you scream.

—That's not what I mean. I want to really scream. I want to scream like I can't help it. I want you to make me scream even though I don't want to.

I thought I knew what she meant. Seeing her legs as she did that handstand in our gravel driveway—the last thing in the world I wanted was to stop seeing her. But I had. It was like I'd gone blind for a second. I saw that she wanted to scream like that.

—So why don't you? she said. Why don't you make me scream?

—Well, I will, I said. Wait here. Just wait.

∎

I went outside. I didn't know for sure exactly what I was going to do. But I thought I knew how to make her scream.

It was a cloudy day. Clouds would cover the sun and then go away. It was hot, sticky.

There was an old hoe against the Tammerand's garage. It had hard mud crusted on its edge. I lifted it up. It was heavy. Good and heavy.

I stopped myself from asking *ready?* It wouldn't work if she was warned.

I raised the hoe as high as I could. I swung it against the sturdy wood side of our bungalow.

The sound of metal on wood was even louder than I thought it might be. Something fell hard inside.

—Hey! she yelled.

I looked in at her, disappointed.

—You didn't scream.

—Look, you clumsy, she said. You broke your own tea cup and saucer. Now don't you feel like a stupid clod jackass?

She frowned at me so hard her big brown eyebrows almost came together.

—Just wait, I said.

I ran into the house. I fished around in my shoe box of things that didn't go with anything else. Found it! Then snatched up a pack of matches with a picture of an arm making a muscle on the front.

I trotted back out behind the bungalow as quietly as possible. I went to one knee. I held it up. I lit the match.

I always saved the last firecracker. I was never quite sure what I was saving it for. Now I knew. It was for this. It must have always been for this.

I smiled as I lit it. And for once I held it in my hand just the way you weren't supposed to do and watched the fast little fuse. It fizzled out.

■

The nub that was left was too short, but I struck the second match, held, and threw.

It landed just inside our front door and exploded.

The noise startled me. So much silence around such sudden sound.

—Oh! Oh!

Sharon came running out. She hit her head on the doorway.

—Look! Look what you made me do!

She held her finger out for me to see.

She'd cut it open along the tip for an inch or two.

—What happened?

—Your stupid firecracker scared me and I hurt my hand on your stupid damn rusty table.

The table we'd saved from the neighbor's garbage was our pride and joy. We ate at it and played cards on it. It was rusty from being left out in the rain before we saved it.

—I should go to the doctor, Sharon said. I should get a shot.

—It's just a scratch.

—It's *bleeding*. And it's more than a scratch. I could die from all the germs. Why did you have to bring that dumb old table inside anyway? Now everything's too small in there. Just too small, too small in there.

She put her finger to her mouth and her face down into her arm. I knew her. I knew pain didn't bother her. I knew she was going to look up and laugh in my face. And I was glad.

Then I heard the sounds she made.

—Sharon?

No answer.

—Sharon, are you..?

—Don't be a stupid ass.

—You are. You're crying.

—I'm not. I never cry and you know it. Want to fight about it, jerk-ass?

—

—I'll fight you anytime, I said.

And I'll make you scream that way.

My thoughts were so loud, she had to hear.

I followed her back through the sheet door. Together we turned the rusty table on its side and shoved it against the back wall of our bungalow.

We had two blankets, a blue and a brown, both torn, also saved from the garbage collector. When we read comics or took a nap, we lay on the blankets.

They were better than fighting on the ground because you didn't tear up your knees and elbows. Your clothes didn't get torn as much. The blankets still smelled like something wet and maybe a little rotten but that was okay.

—I didn't cry, Sharon said.

She hit my chest with both hands. Her eyes were wide with anger, as if she really hated me. I thought that would help.

—You cried. You're still crying.

She shouted—almost a scream—and was all over me, pounding my face and body. We tumbled over, wrestling, each trying to stay on top.

Sharon muttered things I couldn't make out. But I knew she meant that she wanted me to take it back.

She was on top of me. She had her fingers dug into one of my wrists. She used the other hand to try to twist my nose. That's when I toppled her over. I pinned her with my shins on her ankles and my hands on her wrists. My weight held her down. I was growing. I was catching up to her.

—Ahhhhssh!

—There! I said. You screamed.

—You're so stupid. That was no real scream. Not a good scream.

I kept her down. I'd won. I smiled to show her it was okay for her to get up.

Her face went dark, really dark.

—You! Make me so mad. Asshole bastard.

I let loose of her. She rolled away

—Sharon?

She didn't move, her shoulders tucked in, her knees bunched up.

—Sharon, are you okay?

She still didn't move.

—You're so stupid, she said.

—Why? Why am I so stupid?

—Because you think when I'm angry at you and make an angry noise that that's.... Hey.

—What?

—Listen.

—Nothing, Sharon. There's...

—The Good Humor man! I've got an idea. I've got money. Come on I'll buy you something and show you how it's done.

We ran down the driveway. The truck had already cruised past. If they didn't see kids, they sped up. We ran as fast and hard as we could and caught him down at the end of the next block.

—Where'd you two come from? said the Good Humor man.

He was bald and his eyes were close together and he watched Sharon in a funny way I didn't like.

Sharon bought us both the Orange Surprise. It was half orange sherbet and half vanilla ice cream.

We held hands as we walked back. We didn't unpeel the colorful wrappers that showed a sun face slurping on a huge ice cream that was bigger than the beach it was dripping on.

—Go slow, Sharon told me in the bungalow. Isn't it good? Doesn't it taste better than anything in the world?

Her eyes glowed somehow. She had a look. Her cheeks were rounder than ever and she wasn't blinking. I could not stop looking at her eyes as I licked my ice cream, one lick on the vanilla side before turning to lick the orange.

I finished first. I started to throw the stick away.

—No, stupid! Why do you think I bought it for you?

—The stick?

—Yes. Now, while I'm still eating mine, I have to see little man.

—Out here? What if there's people around?

—There's nobody around. Do I have to get finger man to get him?

The bungalow was maybe fifteen feet from her back door. Her dad always seemed to come home from the bank at different times. And he always came and got her the second he got home.

I shook my head.

—So, she said. Where is he, the little man? Do you think you can find him?

Sharon finished her ice cream. She watched me very closely as she licked the stick clean.

—Don't want to get him sticky.

—Get who sticky?

—Little man, dummy. See, if we use this stick to hold him up like this... Then take this other stick and...

She pried the other stick from my fist.

—See, the problem with you, the problem with little man, the problem with me screaming or not screaming, is him not growing. Well, we're giving him some help—see?

—This is stupid, I said. I don't want...

—Shut up.

—Please...

—See, he's kind of like a cripple? And these are his crutches? See? Sometimes you need help to grow up big and strong like...

■

150

Little man's improvement made Sharon happy. It seemed like a personal accomplishment for her. And now I saw how it all fit together, like pieces in a puzzle.

—Do you like-me like me?

—I like you. I love you. I like you.

—Does little man like me?

—Yes. He likes you...very much. Very, very much.

I cupped her chin to bring her head closer so I could whisper.

—Sharon? Want to hear a secret?

Her eyes were big as she studied my face.

—Tell me.

—I think he loves you, Sharon. Little man. I really think he does.

I don't think Sharon screamed the way she wanted to. But for the life of me, I don't remember anything except the feeling that the wonder of the world was all around me and everywhere. Everywhere.

"end of innocence?"

NINETEEN

I didn't see it happen. Sharon said that it was her brother Rodney who destroyed it. She said he yelled and swore and said a lot of very mean things about her and about me. He started saying that he knew everything that we were doing. What we did in the bungalow. You think I don't know you're playing doctor? Playing grab-ass? Play hide-the-monkey? That's what Sharon said he said.

She said he had a big knife. It was a knife where the blade jumped out fast if you pushed a button. He cut up our blankets and our comic books and the old pajamas we'd hung on the window as drapes. She said he'd kicked the table to pieces.

He'd tried to burn the bungalow down, but it didn't burn so well.

I went out behind her house that afternoon to see for myself. You could see Rodney's boot prints everywhere. The wood along the back side near the bottom was burned like charcoal. There was nothing left inside.

Out at the curb I found everything back in the garbage that

we'd saved before. The blankets and sheets and pajamas were in strips.

I picked up a piece of pink flannel. I ran it through my fingers. It ended in a jagged cloth point like a spear or sharp stick.

In my mind, I saw Rodney doing this. Making everything turn into this.

Mom was supposed to be home the night before, but she called and said she was delayed. Her mom was still hanging on and they just didn't know, dad told me.

Dad was out of the house. We'd followed him last week and he didn't seem to be going to Mr. Gaylord's anymore, at least not when we looked for him.

So the house was empty for us.

It was a hot, hot day outside. Be we had all the shades down and the house was staying cool inside.

—*Available,* Sharon said. Her new word.

The way she said it made me think of the signs you'd see on motels when you were going from one city to another. Vacancy. No vacancy.

—Come on, she said. There's no time to waste.

We had our lock-picking tools ready. But I think maybe we both knew that it wouldn't be locked.

I turned the handle and mom and dad's bedroom door swung open like a new world we weren't even sure we wanted to know about, let alone enter.

—Come on, silly!

Sharon never called me scared or a coward. She took a lot of pride, I think, in ending that phase of my life. *Silly* was the closest she'd go to referring to the old me who was scared to go out of the house or peek over the top of a sofa.

But that wasn't it—being scared. I felt bad being in mom and dad's bedroom without them knowing it. If the door had been locked and we'd had to work our hard-earned magic, then I think that somehow it would have been okay. Almost. But the door swung open as if it trusted everyone and everything in the world to be good and do the right thing and not even consider coming in here.

—Under the bed!

—What?

I must have looked and sounded very stupid. I felt like I was walking through one of those museum exhibits where there are ropes separating you from the famous rooms with the real furniture and lamps and hand mirrors and pillows and rugs. And somehow I'd gotten on the wrong side of the rope. I was inside with all the precious stuff. And another tour group would arrive in the room at any second.

—Under the bed, Sharon said.

She was being very patient.

—That's where the secret world starts. That's what Daddy showed me when mom... I mean, come on! Like this!

Sharon fell onto her hands and knees and went flat on her stomach. Then she crawled to the lacy blue and lavender bedspread fringe and stuck her head under. Then back out to check that I was watching.

—See? she said. It's like a waterfall. You can't see through it, but it's easy to go through. And when you do, you're in the secret special world!

Sharon crawled under the bed. She was careful to pull her feet, which were way bigger than mine, all the way under so that nothing of her showed through the waterfall fringe. Just like she said.

—Come on.

I crawled across the brown and green carpet, which was pretty dusty and worn. As soon as I get my head under I could see the rug was less worn under there where Sharon was.

—Pull your legs and feet inside too, silly. If someone comes they won't see anything but the waterfall.

I did that.

For a moment we just lay there on our stomachs looking around under the bed and at each other.

—First, we say these words. You have to get them just exactly right or everything will be horrible forever and forever and forever. Ready?

I took a little breath and smiled. A new game! This was even better than I thought. I stopped feeling bad about the door not being locked.

—Ready, I said.

—What we're going to do is a secret, just between you and me and you can't ever tell anyone in the world. No matter what.

I nodded.

—No, Sharon said. You have to say it.

And she repeated the magic words for me. It took a couple times, but finally I got them just right so that we could go on to the next stage of the game.

—Now we look around for some little thing under here that can go into a very special secret place.

—Like what?

—There's always crap—I mean junk—under a bed. Hairpins or q-tips or shoehorns or just about anything.

Sharon and I looked and looked. Turning around and around. Pretty funny if you think about it, because we were kicking each other by accident and getting in each others' way searching a pretty small area.

—Nothing, I said.

Sharon made another little in-place turn—and then another.

—I guess you're right, she said. In my house, there was

always something. Oh, well. I guess it's okay. Even though he always said it was the key to start the secret game.

He?

—Who's he? I said.

Sharon kind of squirmed away from me, which was hardly any distance at all because she was at the end of the bed against the wall.

—That stupid jerk with the red spots who thinks you're such a great baseballer?

Sharon shook her head.

I was glad.

—That jerk brother of yours—Rodney?

—She shook her head slower at first, then harder, looking me in the eye.

—No more questions, she said. If you want to play the secret game, you have to obey all the secrets. Okay?

—Okay, I said.

Sharon took my wrist. She started pulling my hand toward her. I pulled back to show my strength.

—Hey! she said, then whispered —No, like this.

It took her awhile to convince my hand. This wasn't finger man. Finally, she got me to put it where she wanted it.

—Your turn.

I pulled her hand by the wrist.

—What are you waiting for, silly? Remember? The Good Humor man—Orange Surprise?

Well, okay.

I started to see the point of the game.

—Now you have to say the special secret words to go on to the next part of the game.

—Why?

—That's really dumb. *Why?* Because that's how it's played.

This isn't any old ordinary dumb kids' game. This is the.... the secretest secret game of all time. Maybe you're not ready for it.

Her face looked funny, rounder, her lips looked almost like somebody had hit her in the mouth.

Special secret words? I had to think. We had so many. Then it came to me.

—Your Highness, I said, I may be a common man. But if you give the sign, then I will enter the Palace of Always to begin the sharing forever and ever.

Sharon's face was blank.

We still touched each other, but I could see her eyes get a certain distance in them. She said something that was like a hiss or dismissal. She shook her head. Then she looked back at me, her face inches from mine. She smiled, beamed, her lips started moving to rehearse getting it right, just like in the canyon cave, just like all the ripples of our voices going down into that big darkness.

—I will make the sign, she said. Not for you, Granget, for you betrayed me. But I have seen that all humanity should be here, in the Kingdom of Always, all colors, all beliefs, all shapes and kinds, forever.

I clasped her to kiss. Our hands touching each other were pushed together hard.

Sharon gasped away from the kiss. I thought I'd done something wrong.

—Whoa! she said. You're ready.

And so we crept out through the waterfall. The heat from the day seemed to be creeping into the house, but it was still pretty nice inside.

I patted the bed, almost scared to sit on it. It reminded me of a scene in a movie where people were testing for quicksand. We patted the bed quite awhile before pulling back the covers.

With dad sleeping at the desk in his room and sometimes on the sofa or at Mr. Gaylord's, it hadn't been used for weeks.

We pulled back the bedspread.

Sharon hopped up on top. She curled her legs under her. Then she smiled at me and lifted the sheet.

—Well, she said. Here goes.

She got in and pulled the sheet up to her chin.

—These are the coolest sheets I've ever felt.

She smiled with her cheeks and squinted her eyes shut like a little kid. I watched her. She seemed to be going to sleep.

—Sharon?

She turned over on her side and grinned at me like it was all a joke.

—Come on, silly. Get in. Otherwise, what's the point?

It seemed strange to sit on top of my parents' bed. But once I climbed under the sheets, it seemed like any other bed, just bigger.

Except that I was inside it. With Sharon.

I thought I heard something. We'd closed the bedroom door, but it wouldn't lock. I went up on my elbows.

We both had all our clothes on, even our shoes.

—Get down! Sharon said. They'll see you!

—Who?

—They're out there everywhere!

—Did you hear something?

—No. You can't hear them. You can't see them. You just have to keep your head down and under the covers so they won't get you. Okay?

—Okay.

—Spies, Sharon said.

She turned her face around and pushed into my chest.

—Spies everywhere, she said.

—What kind of spies?

—This kind, she said.

She reached down for my ankle.

—Shoe spies, she said.

She took off my shoe and dropped it on the throw rug beside the bed. She was on my dad's side and I was on my mom's.

—And sock spies...and pants spies...

She had strong hands, but after a bit I had to help her even though I was pretending I wasn't.

—And shirt spies...and...

—That's enough.

—Not enough, she said. Not enough. Underpants spies! See!

She pulled them up and showed them like a trophy.

—Underwear! Remember how we used to...

—Yeah, I said. I remember. Look, out! Duck!

Sharon jumped for real.

—Spies, I said. Shoe spies.

She curled around. Her shoes had a buckle that was impossible to undo inside a bed. Sharon had to do it for me. I knew she wasn't happy about that. But I slipped off her socks and showed them like a great prize, waving them in the air and holding my nose.

—Pee-you!

—Oh, pee-you yourself!

It wasn't as easy as she'd made it seem for spies to steal clothes right off a body. The sheets were in the way and the clothes seemed to want to stay right where they were. And the whole body was in the way, too, with its weight and size and length and all the space it took up in the bed. Sharon's, I mean.

—Well, I guess I won, she said.

—You didn't win. You didn't win anything. My spies are just as good as yours! Better maybe!

I knew they weren't, but it had to be said.

—Well, they're not too bad, I guess, but you should have brought more of them. You forgot to bring your underpants spies. You didn't bring them, so I win.

—You don't win.

—So? Where are they?

The underpants spies went to work. Sharon didn't help them much, just a little.

When the spies first went to work, I had thought about the trophy idea. But by the time I had the underpants off and up, all I could do was look at them.

The elastic at the waist was amazing. It was so tight I didn't know how anybody could breathe wearing them. And the shape of them was so different, so slim and skinny so that they just stuck inside you.

—Go ahead, Sharon said.

She looked at me in a funny way. She seemed interested in my curiosity over her underpants.

—Go ahead and do whatever you want with them.

What did I want to do?

I put them on my face. I made a mask. I could actually see Sharon through it!

—See? I'm the best spy in the world.

—You're a stupid spy. You don't know how to find anything.

I thought I had done so well.

—I found these, didn't I? I made them a mask. What did you do?

—Everything, she said. Everything. You're so stupid and dumb. You don't know anything at all.

I turned away. I looked around the room. My parents' bedroom. There was a dresser with a mirror and pictures around it. Pictures of mom and dad. Pictures of mom with me when I was little. Pictures of my grandparents and my aunts and uncles. Pictures of mom and dad and me when we got together after dad got back from being away.

The floor creaked. It always creaked. The house was so old.

There was a little lamp in the corner that made a nice yellow light and I wished I'd turned it on. But I didn't want to get up to do it.

Sharon nudged me.

—So, you think you're a great spy?

—Sure, I said.

—Then let's have a contest. Let's see who's really the best spy in all the world. See, I've got this finger man spy who can go into your ears and—nope, nothing in there—around your head—knock, knock—that's empty, too. And down here—what's this? You have two ninnies just like me, except mine are bigger and prettier than yours. And this dumb-looking belly button here, I wonder where it goes...

—Stop that—tickles!

—Hmmmm. Must be treasure buried in there he doesn't want me to find. But I'm the greatest spy in the world, I'll come back for it later. I'll go down this path. Hmmm, nothing but a stupid foot down there. And this other one. Same thing. Stupid smelly foot. I guess I have to step off the path, go straight down from the stupid belly button and... What did I tell you? Greatest spy in the whole wide world. I found the little man without any help from anyone!

—I'll bet I could do just as well!

—Never mind. You'll get your turn later. Some day. Some time. Meanwhile, here's the deal.

—

Sharon used her arms and shoulders to flap up the sheet so that it was a kind of tent she could burrow under.

—Here's the thing about this little man. I've suspected him for a long time.

—He's not suspicious, I said. He's just little. Until you start doing that stuff with popsicles.

—Shut up, Davy. He's very suspicious. Why did he stay small for so long? Why did he always pretend he couldn't grow? Why did he hold out on us? I think I know the reason.

—What's the reason?

—The little man is a commonist. I'm going to ask him questions. I'm going to make him talk. I'm going to make him admit that he's nothing but a darned old commonist.

Some months past I had seen the correct word written down and figured out how to say it. I heard it on the radio. I told Sharon how to say the word. But she wouldn't say it. Even on those days we went down into the cave inside the canyon and yelled out over the edge. She said that the word I said was something different. It was *their* way of throwing us off the track, of tricking us into investigating the wrong thing.

It was funny that whenever I heard her say *commonist*, it made me feel like I wanted to keep her safe. And also I wanted to believe it was something we had discovered that was special and secret and that we were the only ones smart enough not to be fooled. But I didn't believe it, not really. And that made me want to protect Sharon even more.

—Do you think he's got the guts to answer my questions?

I tried not to laugh.

—Maybe, I said.

—All right, then. Little man?

—Yes, world's greatest spy?

Sharon was very good at his voice.

—

She shifted her shoulders happily under the sheets.

—Little man, why did you pretend that you could never grow?

—Well, you see, I'm a pretty little man. But I've got big secrets.

—But why did you keep secrets from me? We're supposed to be on the same side. Aren't you on the side of the world's greatest spy with the other good guys?

—Well, sometimes, I guess. But not always.

—Then you admit that sometimes you're on their side?

—Well, I wouldn't say exactly on *their side*.

—Tell the truth! Are you sometimes on their side or not?

—Well, maybe. Yes, I guess sometimes I am.

—Then you are! You are! You are a commonist!

—I'm not! I'm not!

—Look at you. You can't help it. You're showing who you really are! You're showing what you've been hiding all along!

—No! No!

—Oh, yes! And now you're really in trouble. Because we've made a deal with our friends—and now, here they come to get you.

The cannibals!

—No! No! Please great spy, no!

—Cannibals! Cannibals! Cannibals!

They came upon us. The cannibals.

I closed my eyes.

Little man was lost, as good as dead. A total goner.

It was perfection. It was—

The bedroom door.

It clicked open.

My eyes jumped open at the sound.

—Davy?

Mom looked so pretty in her grey traveling suit with the red scarf.

Sharon jumped up from under the covers.

—Davy? Sharon?

—Hi, mom, I said.

—Oh, she said. Oh, well. I've been gone so long and you've...

Mom turned her head. She seemed to try to look behind her as if she was looking back to the bus depot and her trip and all that had kept her away from us.

—Because I've been...gone.

My mom was in the door of her own bedroom. She seemed frozen there. As if she'd never move. Her face and body were frozen there forever.

What if she stood there forever? What was she thinking? What was I thinking?

—Shut..! I yelled.

She looked down at the rug and shook her head a little as if something just couldn't possibly be right. I thought so too.

—Davy? Why don't you and Sharon get dressed? Please? I guess we're going to have to talk.

She turned to go, but she did not. She seemed so hurt, so wounded by seeing me and Sharon in her and dad's big bed. She seemed hurt and sick in a way that nothing could ever make well again. I had no words for it then—and not for many years. But now I know what I thought I saw in her eyes and in the defeated angle of her elegant body. I saw that I had become like everything else in the world that was ugly and selfish and disappointing and mean. I saw that, at least for a moment, I had not only become that world, but embodied it. She knew now that no one else in the world cared so deeply about everything and everyone as she did.

—

Would she ever go? Would she make us stay here in her bed forever and ever and never leave us alone?

—Shut...! I screamed again.

What did I mean? Shut up? Shut the door? Shut down? I don't know. Before god, I don't know.

Then she left us, left the room, left us alone. I had driven my mother away at exactly the wrong moment.

And oh, how like her it was to close the door so gently, so politely, so that the click could scarcely be heard.

—Mom! Mom!

She'd closed the door between us.

—Mom!

She was gone for good.

I shut my eyes. Sharon grabbed my shoulder with her hands.

I gulped in air. I had been holding my breath again. I wondered if mom was holding hers.

Sharon's breath in my face was sour.

—What, Davy?

I looked up.

Mom had put her head back into the room, her face turned a little sideways.

Maybe she was trying to smile. To me, it looked as if she was trying not to shake her head.

I lifted on my elbows to sit up straight. The sheet fell away and I had to yank it up fast.

—Mom, how's grandma? Is grandma okay?

—She's still alive, if that's what you're asking. And I wish I hadn't...

She pulled her head back. When her face was again framed in the opening, her eyes were almost closed.

—I'm only home for a day, Davy. For part of a day. That's all. That's all.

-

TWENTY

School started the next week. Mom was gone again back up north to look after my grandma. We didn't talk about what had happened. I didn't ask mom if she said anything to Mr. Tammerand.

Sharon didn't go back to school. The first day I waited for her to walk with me, but she didn't come out onto the porch. I saw her that afternoon. She was out on her front lawn beating an old orange throw rug with the handle of a broom.

—I'm not supposed to talk to you right now, she said.

She took the throw rug and broom handle and went back into the house.

I saw her two more times after that. She said the same thing, word for word, each time.

A *For Sale* sign went up in front of her house. In a month, she was gone. She did not say goodbye or leave a note or message.

I knew I'd see Sharon again. It turned out I was right.

—

Why did they move away? I doubted that my mother told Mr. Tammerand about catching us in her bed. She had talked to him that once and come back shaking her head, mad. Could Sharon have told her father? Maybe she'd been afraid that my mother would tell and thought it would go easier if she told first. Or maybe Sharon's damn brother bluffed her, the way he had with the bungalow. Maybe she felt she had to tell.

Or was it just coincidence that the Tammerands moved away then? Dad told me that Sharon's father now had a job in Ventura, quite a few miles away, too far to drive every day. So they had to move. But if that was true, then why wouldn't Sharon talk to me? Why couldn't she walk to school with me and pal around with me afterward like we'd always done? I wouldn't have minded if we had to play cards in the same room as her father, with him watching us. I wouldn't have minded anything so long as we were together.

I hated school as much as ever.

I went back to being sick a lot of the time.

Still, without mom home to read to me, it wasn't the same. Dad was there sometimes, but he wasn't much company. I don't think he was writing very much. I never heard the typewriter anymore, even when he closed and locked himself behind his door.

After a while dad started leaving the house in the morning and not coming home until it was time for dinner. He told me himself that he wasn't going to Mr. Gaylord's house.

I kept in practice by jimmying his lock when he was gone. It was easy for me now. But there was nothing new there in his room, even though I went over my notes almost every day.

I went to the cave one last time.

I found Sharon's notebook where she'd left it against the

dirt wall under the oak root. It seemed important that she had left her criminal activity notebook. It meant she was coming back. And the more I went over her files and compared them with mine, the sooner she'd come back.

With mom gone, I made my own breakfast and lunch. I called school a couple times when dad was out, but they said an adult had to do it.

During the day I read *Lassie Come Home* and *The Black Stallion* and *Journey to the Center of the Earth*. In the afternoon I listened to my cowboy and adventure programs on the radio. None of the stories were written by dad. We didn't have a TV yet and I didn't really want one. I made models of space ships and monsters and painted them and put them up in my room where my dolls used to be.

One day I decided to follow dad to see where he went during the day. I stayed about a half block behind him. It was a cool October day and I wore a sweater and a coat over that. There were clouds and a lot of wind. Dad was in a blue shirt he called a Navy work shirt. He kept his hands stuffed in his pockets and he looked cold. He walked past Mr. Gaylord's house. He didn't even turn to look at it as he went by. He turned left at the corner and walked down two more blocks.

I thought about going back home before I got lost for good. Sharon had always done the pathfinding for us.

There was a small, friendly-looking building on the corner. Axminster Public Library. I remembered. Mom and I went there once and got a card and checked out some books. But I always wanted to keep books that I liked and would never let her take them back.

Dad went inside.

I stayed out.

I found a place on a green bench near a bike rack. From there, I could look in through the side window without much chance of being seen.

Dad sat at the end of a long table near the book stacks. He was close to the window. He had several books on the table in front of him and he opened them all. After a few minutes, he looked away from the books. He stared out the window. I thought at first he knew I was there. But then I saw where he was looking. A cherry tree that grew up higher than the library had lost almost all its leaves, but a few little brown ones hung on in the wind. He seemed to be looking at that tree and those quivering leaves.

It was cold on the green bench where I sat, but I didn't really notice it because I was trying so hard to figure out what dad was thinking while he was sitting there staring out the window.

A young man who seemed to know dad came over to him. They talked for a few minutes though the man didn't sit down. They shook hands. Then they both put their fingers to their mouths at the same time to tell each other to be quiet. Maybe the librarian yelled at them for talking. My dad looked at his books for a moment or two, then went back to studying his tree.

After he didn't move a long time, I got up off the green bench and walked home. I didn't know for sure what I was feeling. I knew I was sad for my dad for some reason. And I was sad for myself. But I was feeling something else, an empty kind of thing, that I had no words to express.

Once dad went to school to get my classwork. Once they sent the school nurse to our house. She actually took my temperature and made me say *ahh*. She got mad and threw the homework and the book she'd brought with her down on our sofa. The work sat there. I didn't do any of it. It sat there in a pile on the kitchen sink. I didn't want it in my bedroom.

About a week later dad handed me the local section of the Axminster newspaper. There was an article he wanted me to read. We were sitting at the kitchen table eating the last of our Cherrios from the big yellow box.

Former Cowboy Actor Deemed `Cooperative' by Committee

(AP, with contributions by Dale Forrester, special to The Axminster Gazette)

Tom Gaylord, an actor featured in over 80 B-budget Western movies in the 1930s and 40s before being blacklisted, testified before the House Committee on Un-American Activities Thursday. According to members of the committee, Mr. Gaylord's testimony was "friendly and cooperative."

"He did not take the fifth once, a precedent which more of his fellow actors and other Hollywood types should learn to follow," Dan Gardener, one of the committee's senior members, told this reporter.

The story went on to say the names of some of the movies Mr. Gaylord had starred in like *Somewhere in Santa Fe* and *Texas Avenger*. It said that a couple of his wives were actresses.

I looked at my dad. He had a little smile on his face that didn't seem right at all.

—Are they investigating Mr. Gaylord, dad?

—Yes, Davy. They've been investigating him for years. Years and years. He was one of the first men in Hollywood to be blacklisted. Do you know what that is?

I told him I didn't know.

—Well, son, that's when they put your name down on a list

-

and send it around to all the different studios that make movies. If your name's on that list, no one will hire you. No one will let you make movies anymore.

—That's mean, I said.

—Yes, Davy. It is. It truly is. Worse yet, the list isn't always written. Sometimes it's verbal. Hearsay. I hear your name's on the list, or *might be on the list,* so I'm scared to hire you just in case it *might* be there.

—Do they have the same thing with radio, dad?

—Well...

My dad's face looked kind of like it did in the library when he was staring at the tree.

I wanted to tell him that I had followed him that day.

He looked out our kitchen window toward the backyard where the little broken down garage was with no car in it. I looked too.

—Dad, do you think you'll get in trouble? Do you think you're going to get blacklisted like Mr. Gaylord?

His eyes brightened and he looked me right in the eye, smiling.

—If you tell the truth... If you tell the truth, it doesn't matter what they do to you. If they blacklist you or put you in prison or shut you up permanently. If you tell the truth, you can live with yourself. You can live with yourself and look at yourself in the mirror and you can sleep at night. That's something these committee members can't do. Right, Davy?

I was so encouraged to see him perk up like this.

—Right, dad!

But didn't dad always tell the truth? He seemed to. And shouldn't that make him happy? He didn't seem to be happy, not really. Why hadn't telling the truth made him happy? It's a question I'm glad I didn't ask him.

—

TWENTY-ONE

It was a rainy day when the man came to our door.

I loved the rain. I loved to sit on the sofa in the living room and look out at the front yard with the rain falling. I liked watching it hit the window. It took awhile for the whole square of the window to get wet. But once it all got wet, then when each new drop hit it made a path down through the moisture. Each path was different. I'd watch a drop hit and I'd follow its path. Sometimes I'd listen to the radio while I watched the rain on the window, but not that day.

There was a knock on the door.

I was in my pajamas. I opened the door just a little.

There was a man in a blue suit standing there on our porch folding up a black umbrella. He had on a blue tie. Once he'd finished folding up his umbrella, he put it down on the porch with the point down leaning against the outside corner of our door. He took out a little black notebook.

—Hello, son. Is your father home?

—No. Dad's not home.

—

—Your mother?

—No. My grandma's real sick and mom's taking care of her.

—I see. This is the Graham DiGiorgio residence, is that correct?

—Yes.

I tried to keep the excitement out of my voice. Something about this man reminded me of certain radio shows where detectives stepped in and caught the bad guys and set the good guys free. Maybe this man could help dad stay off this blacklist. Dad said you could never beat the black list, that it just got longer and longer. But there was something about this man in the dark blue suit and blue tie.

—And you're the son? Your name?

I told him my name. I had already made my decision.

—David, tell me, where is your father right now?

I could see the man wanted to smile, but he fought it off. It was amazing how dry he was. The umbrella was very big and he had used it to keep the water off himself, of course, but even his shoes were dry. It was amazing.

—I'm not sure where dad is. He might be at the library over that way a couple blocks. Or over at Mr. Gaylord's house.

The big man wrote in his little black notebook.

—*Tom* Gaylord?

—Right!

I knew that if things went right this could be the beginning of everything getting straightened out for dad. And for mom, too. She wanted my dad to be happy more than anything.

—Well, thanks, son. I guess I'll come back tomorrow when your father's home.

He reached down and carefully grasped his big black umbrella by the handle. *Wait, wait!* I wanted to say. The man opened the umbrella up before he started to step off the porch.

—Sir?

He turned and gave me a funny look. Detectives are always suspicious of everybody so I figured that it was okay.

—Can you help my father?

He undid his umbrella again, very slowly and carefully. He completed the process without any rushing at all. Then he turned to me.

—I'd like to help your father, son. But first I'd need to know just what it is that he needs help with.

I knew it! I knew that all the work that Sharon and I had done would pay off! We'd worked so hard to keep good, clear notes just like adults would do. We'd tried so very, very hard to make them real.

—Could you wait here just a second? I said. Just one second please!

I didn't wait for an answer. I ran to the back of the house where my bedroom was. I dove down on my stomach and fished under my bed and got out the Monopoly board box with no game inside. Inside were all our notes, mine and Sharon's, everything we'd learned and guessed about Mr. Gaylord and dad and Rodney. I jammed the notebooks, hers and mine, under my arm.

I ran back through the house.

The man wouldn't be there. I was just a kid. And he was an important detective with bigger and better things to do than stand on a front porch in the rain waiting for a kid who was still in grammar school to bring him something so he could help out his father.

But he was there. The man in the blue suit was there. He was there exactly as he'd been when I left him.

And I knew the words I had to say to make him know I was more adult than I looked and that what I had to show him was serious and real.

—

—Won't you please come in? I said.

—Well, usually if there's only a minor at home, we..

—Please! Please, I have things I have to show you. I mean, you must see them! I know that if you just come in you can help my father. Please?

I hadn't noticed that the man was wearing a black hat over his black hair until he took the hat off and carried it inside with him. He left the umbrella outside.

—Sit, please, I said. You can sit in dad's chair.

I showed him the big armchair dad liked to sit in.

—Here, I said.

I pushed the notebooks into his hands. I'd taken off the colorful folders that said Head Inspector Investigating Kit and Buster-You're-Under-Arrest Official Crime Station so that he wouldn't think this was play and not take our work seriously. I had slipped out Rodney's file. The truth was that I knew Rodney had nothing to do with anything any adult would care about.

The man in the blue suit handled our notebooks very carefully, almost too carefully. You'd think the president or somebody had given them to him. Still, I liked it that he was so careful. He turned the pages slowly. But it also made me think that nothing we'd put down there could be good enough for such an important detective to spend so much of his time on.

It took him so long to read over our notebooks that I began to think he was trying to figure some nice way of saying that it was useless. He couldn't help my dad no matter how many notes Sharon and I had written down about what he and Mr. Gaylord did.

—This is very interesting, he said. These are copies, of course...

—Yes!

—And very good copies they are, David. Very well done. I see that some of these are by—

—Sharon Tammerand! My friend. My best friend! She used to live next door. Just until a couple months ago.

—I can't say that hers are of much use to us.

The man in the blue suit turned a page over on his lap, then turned it back.

—The misspellings and—oh, well, I suppose we can get around that. And this Gaylord stuff's already in the files...

He sounded like my dad talking to himself. Getting ready to explain why we couldn't buy something or go to a movie.

—But, David, did you say that you'd like to help your father?

I couldn't believe things had turned out so well! The moment I dreamt was actually here. This man was going to help my dad get back to his writing and make us happy again.

—Yes, I said as calmly as I could. Yes, I really want to help my father.

—David, do you think you could get me the original documents from which you copied these notes? Are they in your father's handwriting?

Hooray! I almost blurted out. But I didn't want to make him mad so that he'd go away and not help us.

—Yes. Yes, I can, I said. My dad keeps his room locked, but I know *exactly* how to get in! Come on. Come on!

—Son, I can't get involved in...

—Please! Please! It's so easy. I want to show you how Sharon and I always do it. Dad doesn't even know. He's never even guessed!

I ran to the den. I watched over my shoulder to make sure the big man in the blue suit followed me. He was doing something strange with his notebook, flipping its pages like you would do with a deck of cards.

I knelt at the door. The big man came up behind him.

—It's easy! I just...

—

—I can't authorize you to do this. If you do open this door, you do so of your own volition and free will. Is that understood?

I told him it was all okay. Everything was okay.

Out of my pocket I took mom's nail file and the skinny piece of metal from grandpa's tool box. I kneeled down. I fit the stiff strips into the lock and turned.

Nothing.

I tried again.

Nothing.

I started to sweat. Had dad changed the lock? I said something up to the man in blue, but he didn't seem to hear. He was losing interest with every second I wasted. He was so tall, so impossibly far above me where I kneeled on the floor. I never wanted anything so badly as I did to show that man how I could get into that locked room and give him the original documents that he needed to help my dad.

But I couldn't. No matter how hard I tried, I couldn't.

—I'm sorry, son. I have to go now.

—Oh, please! Listen! I wasn't lying! Honest, I...

—It sounds like telling the truth is important to you, David.

He was walking away. Already he seemed almost gone from us. Forever.

—Sir, it's important to me. And it's way, way more important to my dad. Telling the truth is the number one thing with him. The number one thing.

The man in the blue suit reached our front door. He turned back to me.

—I believe you, David. I believe that you want the truth to come out so that we can save your father from whatever it is he's got himself into.

I wanted to go down onto my hands and knees and bow to this man.

—

—Now, I can't authorize you to do anything illegal. Do you understand that, David?

I nodded. I really did understand.

—But if somehow you should come by the documents we discussed, then I might find some use for them that would help the truth come out about your father. How does that sound to you?

—Great! I said.

—Then, I'll be back the same time Thursday. Will that work with your schedule?

Oh, would it! And I made him see that I really meant it, too. And I thanked him—oh, how I thanked him!

I closed the door, but I couldn't help but push the side curtain away and watch as the man in the blue suit put his black hat back on. He opened up his umbrella before he stepped off the porch.

It was hardly raining at all now.

I noticed that the detective hadn't parked his car in front of our house. It was down past the Tammerand's, just like in the movies.

Everything Sharon and I had worked for was finally paying off.

I sat down on the sofa. I didn't think about the rain.

Then I started to wonder. If you were an important man in a beautiful blue suit with a beautiful black umbrella and black hat and notebook and a kid jabbered away at you and said he could get a door open—and then he couldn't even do that one little thing, couldn't get it open—what would you think? Wouldn't you think the kid was just playing around, maybe not lying on purpose, but really just making it all up?

Yes, if you were such a man, that's just what you'd think.

I went back to dad's door. Why would he change locks? Maybe because of something in Mr. Gaylord's article, that business about being *friendly and cooperative*? I didn't under-stand.

I put in the tools and twisted. No, but...

...and it opened. Just like that. The lock opened.

Why couldn't I do it with that man there who needed me to do it? Why couldn't I open it when I was supposed to?

Well, he said he'd be back on Thursday. I'd just have to wait. But I'd have to leave everything in there until I was sure dad was out of the house that day, if he left at all.

Or should I tell dad about the man who might try to help us? Would dad understand or think it was just one of my kid's games?

My father was obviously a very special person; at least, so I've been told. In the intervening years, I've met more than a few adults who were present as children when doors were knocked on in the late 1940s and early 50s. Most watched a parent answer. Some went to the door with mom or dad, their faces half-buried in dresses or trousers. A few, like me, were alone. But each and every one of them has laughed at me. Each and every one of them has recited from memory the words imprinted into their brains by fathers and mothers in anticipa-tion and apprehension of that dire knock. *Do not under any cir-cumstances speak to or communicate with in any manner whatsoev-er any person who should come to the door dressed in a...*

No, I had never heard from my father's lips any words even vaguely resembling these. They laughed at me, but he was the one they were calling names. Quixote. De Bergerac. Fool. These were the sorts of pronouncements I have heard leveled at my father for his oversight.

Some oversight. And what is it, one wonders, that they call the son of such a fool?

But there is an appalling consolation, if one really feels the need to search it out. Because, here at the end of this sad century, at the end of this calamitous millennium, one strongly suspects that one may, in fact, turn out to be something much worse than a fool.

As Thursday approached, I became quite certain that the man in the blue suit would not return. Why should he come back simply to humor an over-imaginative child?

And so that morning I waited for dad to leave the house. I did not follow him. Maybe he went to the library. Or maybe he was visiting Mr. Gaylord again now that Mr. Gaylord's eighth wife had moved out for the second or third time. Or maybe dad was somewhere else, walking, sitting.

It didn't matter to me. The only thing that mattered was that I had the chance to help him.

Thursday morning. His door was locked. I started to open it. No.

It was exactly like before, when the man in the blue suit stood over me watching me fail to do the thing I said that I could do. The tools didn't work. I couldn't make them work.

It was exactly the same. And I knew that he was coming soon.

And so I thought of Sharon. That always helped me. What would Sharon do?

She would laugh and make a game of it and it would— open.

Yes, it did. I ran into my dad's room. The papers were there. Everything was there. Exactly as yesterday, when I'd done my dry run. And I grabbed up everything just as the man in the blue suit had said I should.

All off the record, of course. Just like in the movies. And

that was all right. Because I understood that sometimes good things can only be done by doing them *off the record*. Didn't all the heroes in all my favorite movies work that way?

So it was true that I was a hero. A little one, but a real hero.

Because I knew the big hero was the man in the blue suit.

If he would only come as he said he would.

He said the same time Thursday. The time was past. But I knew he had other detective work to do. And so I tried my best to be patient.

The sun was out today. That seemed a bad sign. It seemed like maybe if it was raining, then he would be the same and take me seriously again like he had before.

I thought about Sharon and I thought that if the man came back today then Sharon was sure to come back someday, too.

I tried to listen to the radio.

I tried to read.

I tried not to think about waiting for him.

Then it was the time when my dad usually came back from wherever he went. And then I saw it. I knew exactly what was going to happen. The man would come and my dad would return at the same time. My dad would not understand that the man had come to help him—no matter how hard I tried to convince him. Everything would be ruined. Our family would never be happy again.

There was a knock on the door.

I opened it.

The man had on the same dark blue suit, but he wasn't wearing his black hat and of course he didn't have an umbrella. But he already had his notebook in his hands.

—Hello, David, he said. Is your father home?

It was like a code we'd made up between us.

—No. My dad's not home.

—Your mom?

—No.

—Did you find anything around the house that you want to show me? Something that you'd like to turn over to me for a few minutes of your own free will?

—Yes, I said. Here.

I handed over all the papers. Most of them were in dad's handwriting. But others were letters from people to dad that had to do with clubs and meetings and places to meet.

The man looked at them.

—Okay, he said. Here's what's going to happen. I'm going to be gone about an hour. When I come back, I'm going to give all this back to you. Davy, do you know what you're going to do then?

I had no idea.

—You are going to put everything back exactly as you found it. Do you think you can do that?

I nodded. I knew I could! Sharon and I had studied dad's room inch by inch! We knew the exact place for everything of dad's.

—I'll be back in an hour. After that, you and I will have a secret. The secret is that I was never here. You do really want to help the truth come out about your dad, right?

—Yes! I said. It's what I want. It's what dad wants.

The man in the blue suit looked uncertain about that.

—Good, he said.

He was back in an hour. I had dad's room open and ready and simply slipped everything back into place. Exactly.

Five minutes later, dad came home.

—You hungry, Davy? What do you want for dinner?

It was exactly like in the movies. I'd gotten in under the wire. Just in the nick of time.

It felt so right. It felt so perfect. So truly perfect. So I was the hero after all!

—

TWENTY-TWO

The next week mom came home for good.

—Grandma's fine, she said. The doctors say she's getting better. How are you and your father, Davy?

—Fine, mom.

—How are you really?

I wanted to tell her about the man in the blue suit who took dad's papers away for a short time.

—We're okay I guess.

—Really?

I closed my eyes while I nodded that it was really all okay.

—You miss Sharon, don't you honey? Well, you'll see her again someday, I'm sure. Maybe... Well, maybe it was for the best.

Her words hurt. But that was okay. She didn't mean for them to hurt. She meant well.

It was so good to have her back. She read me *Treasure Island* and *Kidnapped*, just like when I was little and frightened by everything outside the pages of those wonderful books.

—

I went back to school. I had no idea what was going on in class because I hadn't done the work. I'd hid all the papers and books when mom came back so that she wouldn't ask me about my assignments. Since I couldn't do the new work in math or science or social studies, I went over in my mind everything that Sharon and I had done and enjoyed doing, all the adventures we'd had together.

It was after Thanksgiving but the weather was hot again. Mom was cooking dad's favorite dinner with eggs and hot dogs cut up with different kinds of spicy sauce mixed in. It was too hot in the house and I told mom I was going for a walk.

She looked surprised.

—How nice! she said. Davy.

It wasn't a question, but she was looking at me with a strange smile so I stopped in my tracks.

She wiped her hands on her apron and smoothed back her hair. She was sweating a little on her forehead.

—You're going to be okay now, aren't you?

She wasn't asking me. It was like she was deciding this for herself.

—You're really going to be okay now, aren't you?

—Yes, mom.

I almost ran out of the house. It was like my mom was in my mind. Like she knew that I'd decided just that minute to go back and visit our good old places. I started out with the bungalow, what was left of it. I walked around to the side of the house and sat on the electric meter and pretended I was dead. I brought myself back to life. Not much fun. I opened the heavy cellar door and let it slam shut. That felt good. Then I walked down the street past the school and finally ended up at the canyon.

—Hello?

Something was trying to answer.

—Hello, Sharon? Are you there?

I went blank when someone else who wasn't really there at all picked up a rock and threw it into the canyon. The sound of something thrashing, fighting, rushing through the grass and brush that had started growing again with the rains.

—Sharon? Sharon? Is that you?

I listened.

—Tell me when you're coming back. Please tell me.

When I got back home I almost didn't go inside. It was awful hot in there and the smell was really bad.

In the kitchen I saw the skillet black with eggs and burned up hot dogs with smelly hot sauce black all over the sides and bottom.

I thought I heard mom in the bathroom. There was a sound like a little cat or dog whimpering like someone had hurt it.

Dad sat at the kitchen table. I never saw him look like that. He looked bigger and meaner than I had ever seen him. But he looked smaller too in a way I couldn't explain.

He had an envelope in his hands. It was a long envelope with typing and it had his name on it. I could see that he had torn it open. I didn't see any stamps on the envelope.

—Dad, the mailman came three hours ago? What is that? A mistake or something?

Dad looked up at me. He looked me in the eye. His eyes looked like a man on a show we'd watched once on the Tammerand's TV and mom said she'd never let me see again. Everything was dark except for the man's face and bald head and his eyes were horrible.

—It's not mail, he said.

—Then...then what is it, dad?

—A man came to the door. A Negro man. That's how they do it now, you know. A nice-looking Negro man in a blue suit. He put it in my hand. I smiled and took it. I took it without

—

looking. I took it from him to show that I trusted him because we were both human beings.

I had never thought about my heart beating in my chest. Never before that moment. I felt the thump. It felt like whatever it was that was in there wanted out.

—A subpoena. I'm subpoenaed to their god-damned committee.

I looked all over the kitchen really fast, but there were no answers. What had I expected?

—Dad, I'm sure everything'll be okay. I'm sure they only want to help. As long as you tell...

My dad put his head down in his hands. He put his head down in his hands and said something. Even though his wrist was caught up in his mouth I heard what he said.

—Fuck, he said. Oh, fuck.

A few weeks after Christmas I saw some teenagers driving down the street in a dirty white convertible car with the top down. The sun was out and the weather was warm and nice, so it wasn't strange that their car was open.

Something caught my eye.

I thought the boy in the passenger seat looked like the boy with red splotches on his face who said he liked to watch Sharon playing baseball.

I looked at the kids in the back seat. The boy was skinny and tall and older and looked kind of familiar.

Then I saw Sharon.

At least, I thought it was Sharon. She was kind of slouched down in the seat. Her face was against the tall, skinny boy's chest as if she was using him to sleep on. Except her eyes were open and she was smiling.

Then the car turned the corner and was gone.

I thought it was Sharon, but it couldn't be. She lived in Ventura, which was pretty far from here. And if she came back to Axminster, I knew she'd come back and visit me.

Almost every month now dad was getting letters that made him happy. For a day or two at least. Then he got really upset and angry all over again at the waiting. The meeting he was supposed to have with that committee had to be moved back because things were going slowly. No one seemed to have time for my dad. And that made him feel good, it seemed. At least for a day or two.

I began to wonder if the kind of help the man in the blue suit wanted to give my father was the kind of help he really needed.

TWENTY-THREE

—I have a surprise for you today, honey.

Mom was smiling her most glorious smile. She smiled that smile when she thought that something was going to make me or dad really happy.

—We're going to dress you up in your best clothes.

—Why, mom?

—You'll see, honey. You'll see!

Dad wasn't home. But he had stopped going to the library and he couldn't go to Mr. Gaylord's house anymore because Mr. Gaylord was gone. One of his daughters by his second wife had come and taken him. She wanted him to live with her. It sounded to me like something you'd do with a child. I wondered if Mr. Gaylord's daughter felt like she had to do something like that because her father wasn't very tall, that he was kind of short, like a child.

So I didn't know where dad was.

But mom watched me every step of the way as I dressed.

She smiled and helped me straighten my pants and shirt and get my socks on straight.

—Mom, this is ridiculous.

—You're going to want to look your best, Davy. You're going to want to look perfect.

—Why?

The new family who had moved into the Tammerand house was gone now, too. And after I got to looking as perfect as mom felt I could look, she started staring out the window in that direction, watching the Tammerand house, waiting for something.

It was the kind of day that Sharon and I hated. It was warm and somehow it seemed dark indoors. It was the kind of day you just had to go out from under the ceiling and away from the walls. You had to go out into the air, out under the light from the sky.

We seemed to wait forever. Whatever the surprise, it couldn't be worth this wait in these clothes that I hated to wear. I knew I looked stupid in these clothes that were worse than school clothes. I just wanted whatever this was to be over.

Mom jumped away from the window.

—They're here, Davy. Are you ready?

I was, as far as I knew.

—Well, let's go!

We went out the front door and headed for the Tammerand house. The family that lived there over the last nine or ten months had left last week and a *For Rent* sign went up on the front lawn. Mom told me that Mr. Tammerand still owned the place. He rented it out to make more money.

I didn't understand why we had to go next door into an empty house. Unless mom wanted us to rent it, which didn't make any sense.

Mom and I went to the front door. Mr. Tammerand opened

▬

it. He was wearing a blue suit very much like the one the man wore who told me that he could help dad. He stepped to the side to let us in, just inside the door, and mom went in and stood beside him.

Somehow I was in the middle of the room.

What in the world was going on? How could mom possibly think that this was a great surprise for me?

—In there, Mr. Tammerand said.

In there what? He wanted me to go in there—or to never, ever, even look in there or think of going in there for the rest of my life?

My mom came closer. She seemed afraid to touch me.

—It's okay, Davy, she whispered. Just go in. It's all right.

I went to the door. It was dark heavy wood. I'd always hated that dark old door. I opened it.

Since the house was empty, there was no furniture, no lights, nothing.

I stepped into the empty room.

The door closed behind me, gently. It must have been my mother. I heard whispers out in the room behind me.

I'd seen movies where kids were punished by being locked away by themselves. For a moment I really did think that it was happening to me. Except why was I all dressed up? And why was my mom letting this happen?

There were two chairs in the room. They were dark wood chairs almost exactly the same color as the door. One was against one wall, the wall toward the rear of the house. The other, facing it, was pulled out two or three feet from the opposite wall.

She was sitting in the first chair, the one against the rear wall next to the window with the closed shades.

Her hands were folded in her lap and she was wearing a horrible dress. She wasn't looking at me. She wasn't looking at

-

anything really, not even her hands. I thought of my father sitting in the library looking out the window at the tree.

—Hello, Sharon said. Why don't you sit down?

I looked at the chair almost all the way across the room from her. I felt stiff in these uncomfortable clothes. I crossed the room and sat carefully.

We both did more or less the same thing.

We didn't stare. We didn't look at each other. We looked kind of away to the side.

The two chairs were the only things in the room. The chairs were real, but not us. I had dreamt of seeing Sharon again, and now here she was across the room from me. But something was very wrong. She didn't seem to really be here. And I was just the same, not there either. I thought maybe it was the room.

The awful afternoon light from our house seemed to have followed me here. Except here in this empty room it was worse. It was grey brown and ugly all over me and her. I could feel it and it seemed to make rules about what happened here.

—Well, Sharon said. I guess we're supposed to talk.

I didn't know what to say. I looked at her dress. It was new. I didn't like it. It had full sleeves and the hem went down almost to her ankles. It was white with small blue, yellow and brown windmills everywhere all over it, up and down.

I stared at those windmills. I just stared at them.

—Well, she said. How are you?

—I'm fine, I said.

—Are you... That is, school. Tell me about school.

I may have answered, but I didn't know what I was saying.

The floors were hard wood. Our chairs were a long way apart. The clothes we wore were clothes you wore when you met somebody for the first time. A little voice in my head said that even if for some reason the chairs could not be made to go closer together, I could go closer. Or Sharon could.

■

I looked at her face. It was different. It was bigger and rounder and yet longer, too. And her eyes were different. There was no sparkle or color in them. I didn't see any of the ideas and plans that were always flying out of her eyes. And for a minute I believed that this was not Sharon but some older sister or someone unrelated who they had made look a little like Sharon.

But why would they do that?

I knew it was her. But it was not her, too.

I kept thinking about going down on the floor in these stupid stiff clothes, going down on the floor right there at the foot of her chair. Right there at her feet.

—Do you have new friends? she said.

—Yes, I lied.

—Do you do lots of stuff at school and stay busy all the time?

—Yes.

We looked at each other. Then we looked away. Sharon shifted in her seat.

Something was happening. She was uncomfortable in the dress. She fussed and squirmed in the chair. She twisted her head around.

Oh, she was going to come out of that dress just to show me it was her, not for any other reason than to show me it was her and that we were still Sharon and—

—I'm sorry, she said.

She had stopped shifting around and folded her hands again. She was looking at me with an expression on her face that I could not figure out.

—I'm sorry, she said.

I didn't say anything. I was still hoping we could go back to the moment when we were almost ready to be ourselves again.

Yes! She shifted. She was uncomfortable, too!

—

—I'm sorry, she said. What was your name again?

I sat back in the hard chair. I could do that. I could sit there. I could sit there in this horrible empty room for as long as I was supposed to do it.

I think I must have told Sharon my name.

I know that there was silence. There was a lot of silence that went on for quite a while.

—Well... she said later on.

A little after, the door opened.

My mom poked her head in.

—Well, did you two kids have a nice...a nice talk?

I could not look my mom in the face. I couldn't look anybody in the face.

Mom came a little into the room. I think she felt it a little, what a horrible room it was, and how horrible it would be to be with anyone in a room like that with that horrible afternoon light coming into it.

—I guess we should be going now. Sharon and Mr. Tammerand have a lot of errands to attend to before they go back to Ventura.

Sharon came one step closer.

—Well, goodbye...David.

My name was strange to her and hard for her say. I felt sorry that she had been made to say it.

Years later, I remembered one of my mom's old expressions. She was so generous to everyone. When things turned out badly, perhaps not at all the way someone had intended them to, she would speak of the person as having *meant well*.

In the end, many people were not nearly so generous to my mother as she had been to them. At least, that's how I see it. But regarding this one incident which she apparently initiated and which I will never forget, I know above all that she did in fact mean well.

■

EPILOGUE

Well, there it is. Done. I never would have believed I could remember so much. Never.

Adults are the gods in the lives of children. Seems like I've proved just the opposite. I still can't believe what I did to my father.

I have the FBI files in front of me as I write. I have all the pages they will give out on Graham DiGiorgio, and after special negotiations and a little pressure from a friend, on Tom Gaylord as well.

My father never did officially testify in any public forum. Not for HUAC, nor for anyone else. Others have claimed he did, both in print and around the appropriate circuits of gossip. But I am not a particularly litigious person. And what has been said of my father really doesn't matter any more. Besides, it's not the culpability of others I'm concerned with, but rather my own.

Yes, dad did give a series of responses to a stenographer in the employ of the committee. He wasn't defiant; neither was he cooperative. He named no names. Still, dad was small potatoes.

Sharon used Davy as an escape & never really learned his name.

HUAC may have already been starting to understand that America was no longer a hundred percent behind it. To publicly crucify a struggling radio writer? How would that help their image? Well, they did worse with others, even some less prominent than my dad. But I guess our timing was right. The stenographer's material was deemed *inconsequential*; it says so right here. And that's as far as it goes.

Inconsequential.

All they had, really, was his non-religious conscientious objector stance during WWII and the hard time he served for taking that stance. Everything else was deemed "tangential." It seems strange, after all these years, to see copies of the pages I provided the man in the blue suit. I still cannot described how it feels to see these sheets and to touch them.

No, I didn't know what I was doing.

And, of course, it says right here that Thomas Trenton Gaylord was "one of the great singers." Singers, not sinners. The words are penciled in across the cover sheet. No one bothered to erase the phrase before sending me the xeroxed document. I wonder about the authorship of that terse judgement. I wonder if it might have been the chairman himself. I wonder.

Mr. Gaylord named my dad, of course. Mr. Gaylord named everyone. Every name he could conjure—and some with which he needed help. "Oh, oh, yeah! Her, too! Yeah and him!" That's right here in the transcript.

Yes, indeed. A great singer.

Well, I guess he had to be a great something.

Sharon. Have I seen her since that dark afternoon in that empty room in that empty house? Not that I remember. Someone—maybe my mother—told me once that Sharon had married and had children. I don't know. I don't think I want to know.

Not long after, mom and dad and I left Blossom River Drive.

Axminster, California, had not, after all, proved to be that one short step to Hollywood of which my father had dreamed.

Still. Still there must have been lessons learned, concepts acquired. I feel the need to thank the departed spirit of the Senator from Wisconsin. From him, I learned to embrace the great treasure that is mediocrity; I learned to reside, to rejoice, to revel in it. For a quarter century—and more—I have taught high school. Grades, detention, curses, fights, these daily pre-occupations fill one's mind, fill those dangerous places where otherwise new ideas could, like cancer cells, catch hold, take root and grow. I taught novels about perfect fathers overcoming racism in the American south of the late 1930s, that, and other pleasant fairy tales my students knew were lies. I have written nothing but this because I have thought of nothing else.

Thanks to him, too, the not-so-grand-inquisitor, my father learned that it is best to trust no one; even those closest to you may betray your dearest thoughts and feelings. He learned the virtues of isolation and self-enclosure. He learned to have the strength to make the good clean break from sentimental attachments that might prove inhibiting. When he moved away in December, 1953, mom and I were less than surprised because it felt as though he had been gone for many years.

Too, the Senator taught us the value of the created truth; that is to say, the untruth that becomes the accepted reality. Without this special tool, I could not have lived through these years. Without it, I could not have survived those years of my mother's illness. Such a profound and bountiful legacy from our Senator and his minions.

After Aunt so-and-so decided that she had done enough, Kay brought grandma into our house and saw to her—and to my increasing emotional and physical needs—night and day for eight years. "It's going to be all right," I heard mom tell her mother on the last night. If you're going to lie, make it a big one; they just may buy it.

At what seemed like the precise end of this period, the time when grandma finally died, my mother was diagnosed with the same cervical cancer she had observed, hovered over, and tended to for those eight years. It seems like four lifetimes, but I guess it's been less than a generation since the good Senator's invaluable bequest served me in good stead.

I could not bear to see her going through what her own mother had gone through. But I did bear it. And when the time came, and I said the magic words, repeated them verbatim, just as I'd heard her say them, with the same warm, assured intonation, the same loving cadence, my mother had the good grace—a gentle curtsey to our sagacious Senator—to smile and nod and close her eyes forever.

I seem to have had a reader in mind as I composed these pages, an ideal reader. But that's an idea I've now abandoned. There is no "you" to whom I would ever dare to entrust these words. I may be a fool, but I'm not fool enough to make public at this late date a document that would get me yanked out of line and accused of scaring the others.

And so, finally, I guess I'm glad that I've written all this in ballpoint pen in my indecipherable scrawl. Even my mother could not read my handwriting. And certainly no teacher ever could. It's as good as cryptography, like all the various ingenious codes Sharon and I devised together. I can tuck this away in the same drawer with the cherished reports I no longer want. Even if someone found this sad excuse for a memoir, no one would be able to translate a word of it. And so I'm safe.

Despite the voices of children I seem to hear from time to time, echoing, echoing down from some indeterminate point above and beyond my vision. Safe.

I'm safe at last.